ON BEING SARAH

The kitten mewed once more, then climbed right up onto Sarah's shoulder.

ON BEING
SARAH

Elizabeth Helfman

Illustrated by Lino Saffioti

Albert Whitman & Company
Morton Grove, Illinois

The text typeface is Palatino.
Design by Lucy Smith.

Library of Congress Cataloging-in-Publication Data
Helfman, Elizabeth
On being Sarah/Elizabeth Helfman; illustrated by Lino Saffioti.

p. cm.

Summary: Even though life with cerebral palsy isn't easy
for twelve-year-old Sarah, she manages with the help
of her loving family and several new friends.
ISBN 0-8075-6068-5
[1. Cerebral palsy—Fiction. 2. Physically handicapped—Fiction.
3. Family life—Fiction. 4. Friendship—Fiction.]
I. Saffioti, Lino, ill. II. Title.
PZ7.H374On 1993
[Fic]—dc20
92-28167
CIP
AC

*For Kari, without whom this book
could not have been written*

Contents

1

Talk *to* Me,
Not *about* Me!

Sarah moved her wheelchair closer to the big picture window in the Bennett living room. There! She could watch everything that went on in the street. Sarah loved to see how people walked. A man went by briskly, with long, hurried strides. A woman pushing a baby carriage dragged tired feet. A child skipped, laughing. People did this every day, without even thinking about how their legs took them wherever they wanted to go. Well, it would take more than thinking to make *her* legs move. She gave her knee a disgusted poke with her good left hand. Those legs. They looked all right, like anybody's, but they were no use to her, none at all. And they'd been like that all of her twelve years.

Today, Sarah's sister, Amy, just two years older, had

promised to bring home her friend Sue, after they had lunch and a swim at Sue's house. Amy had told Sarah so much about Sue. "She's pretty," Amy had said, "and she's a marvelous swimmer."

It was some time since Amy had brought anyone home. Summer vacation days could be long and dreary for Sarah. There was no school, and her mother was busy with housework.

"Why don't you bring Sue here?" Sarah's mother had asked Amy.

"She wants me to go to her house," Amy said. "Besides, she has a swimming pool."

"Ask her."

"Oh, all right." Amy had seemed uncomfortable with the idea.

She doesn't want Sue to see me. I'm that little sister who has cerebral palsy and can't walk, Sarah couldn't help thinking.

There they were! Amy came walking up the street in her usual sturdy way, now and then tossing her long, dark hair back from her face. *I'd know my sister a mile away,* Sarah thought. The girl beside Amy walked quite differently, putting down each foot daintily, as if the sidewalk might hurt. Her hair was different, too; yellow curls clung close to her head.

Then they were in the house and coming towards her.

"This is my sister, Sarah," Amy said, almost in a whisper, as if she didn't want to say it.

"Hello, I'm Sue," Sue said.

Sarah had never seen anyone so beautiful. Big blue eyes gave Sue's face an expression of wonder, and her skin was soft and pink. Her shorts matched her eyes, and her T-shirt had flowers printed all over its front. Sarah wanted to touch her, but she wouldn't dare.

Sue seemed to be waiting for her to say something.

"My sister can't talk," Amy explained, and Sarah felt Amy didn't want to say that, either.

Sue stared. "Why can't she talk?"

"She was born that way," Amy said.

"That's terrible, not being able to talk. I never heard of that happening to anybody." Sue stood stiff and tense.

"It hardly ever does," Amy said.

Sarah had been through this so many times. People talked about her as if she weren't there, or as if she couldn't hear. Sarah managed to keep from crying out in protest. She didn't want to touch Sue, not anymore. She just wanted to get away from there.

But as she pushed the switch on the arm of her

13

wheelchair and started to move away, Amy said, "Don't go, Squib! I want you to show Sue your symbols."

Sarah let go of her switch. All right, maybe after all, Sue could see she had something to say.

"Look, Sue," Amy was saying. "She has these symbols. If you watch, she can tell you nearly anything without speaking a word."

"Are those the symbols?" Sue asked, looking at the board that covered Sarah's wheelchair tray. It was divided by lines into many small squares. In each square was a drawing made of lines and circles, and above the drawing, a printed word.

"Those are Blissymbols," Amy said.

"That's really neat," Sue said. "Tell me something, Sarah."

Sarah wasn't sure she had anything to say to Sue, after all. She pointed to a single square near the top of the board.

"'Hello!'" Sue was reading the word above the symbol. "How come that says 'hello'?"

"It's a mouth—see?" Amy said. "That little circle. And arrows coming together."

"When arrows go the other way, it means 'good-bye.'"

"That *is* neat!" Sue exclaimed.

Sarah could talk pretty fast with her family and her teachers because they already understood the symbols. It was much slower with someone who had to read the words, too.

She was trying to think of something else to tell Sue when Amy said, "Show her some of the first symbols you learned."

Sarah pointed to "OK," which was printed separately at the top of her board because she used it so often.

house	tree	flower	face
△	⼂	⚲	⏀

"They look like what they're supposed to be!" said Sue.

"Lots of them do," Amy said.

"Why doesn't she just point to words?"

"Symbols are quicker. Besides, when Sarah first

learned them in school she couldn't read."

"Can she read now?"

"Sure. Sometimes she spells out words if she hasn't got a symbol for what she means. See—she has all the letters of the alphabet, there, across the top of the board."

There they were again, talking *about* her as if she weren't there. Sarah had hoped she would have a real conversation with Sue, the way she did with Amy. Maybe they could even play a game together. Now she could see that wasn't going to happen. Oh well, then she wouldn't even listen.

Amy and Sue were talking about playing games at school. Sitting right where she was, Sarah took herself away from there, in her mind—as she knew so well how to do. When she was younger and couldn't talk with symbols, she had spent long hours daydreaming, alone in her own world. She could still dream herself away when she needed to.

Now, in her mind, she was back at her old school, where she had learned symbols and so much besides. Every child in her class—there were just six, including herself—was in a wheelchair, and not one could speak clearly enough to be understood. It had been hard at first. They all tried to say things. Instead, they made

16

noises, blinked their eyes, waved their hands, shook heads yes or no—if they could. And the teachers gave them pictures to point to—a glass of water to mean you were thirsty, a sandwich for being hungry, the toilet if you needed that, and so on.

Before she had gone to school, Sarah had not been sure there was anyone else like her in the whole world. A woman named Mrs. Brady had come to the house twice a week to give Sarah exercises, and she used to talk about other children she worked with. These children had never seemed real to Sarah. She had never seen any children like herself. She had been just a baby, even when she was five years old. No one, perhaps not even her parents, expected her to grow up properly. Surely she would just go on making those noises, saying, "Agghh!" when she tried to talk. She would watch the world around her without ever really being part of it. The questions she kept asking inside herself would hardly ever find an answer. She was nobody.

She remembered how it had been when she was younger. There had been so much she wanted to say. Words tumbled around in her brain, waiting to be spoken. She had heard these words a thousand times as her mother said them, her father, her sister—everyone. She could not speak a single word to them. Over and over again she would try to make the sounds to say a word. She would shudder inside when she heard the noises that came out, no words at all. Sometimes she would put her head down on the tray of her wheelchair and cry. There was no way, though, that she could ever stop trying to speak; she was driven.

Then she had learned to talk with symbols. It was like waking up from a long, dim daydream and discovering the world. The thoughts and feelings she had hidden inside herself could come out because, as her teacher said, "Symbols do what talking does." She could ask questions and get answers—what a difference that made!

Of course, she would never get out of that wheelchair, never speak an understandable word with her voice. She knew that. But she was growing up, the way all children do. She was Sarah Bennett, and she was going to be somebody in this world. Going to school and learning symbols meant that much to her.

She knew she would miss the old school, Ingleside. It hurt even now to recall what her friend Paul had said to her in symbols on her last day there: *You are my always friend.* She had gotten her wheelchair as close to his as she could and had given him a hug with her good arm.

Sarah's teacher had told her that Paul's family would be moving to another city. She would probably never see him again.

Now, in a few weeks, she would be going to sixth grade in Jacobson School, just down the street. This was the middle school where Amy had gone before high school. Amy had been eleven years old in sixth grade. Sarah was twelve; getting started in school had been harder for her, so it took longer.

Sarah had chosen Jacobson herself; she wanted to go to a regular school, like anyone else. And instead of traveling a long way from home in a special van, she would go to school by herself, straight down the street in her wheelchair.

Her mother appeared in the doorway. "How about a snack, you three? Sarah and I made chocolate chip cookies this morning."

That was so like her mother, always reminding people that she, Sarah, could do things other people could do. She turned her wheelchair towards the dining area.

Sue was saying, "Mm-mm, that sounds good," as they gathered around the table, Sarah on the side where she could fit her knees underneath.

"Fresh apple juice from Pierce's orchard," Sarah's mother said as she poured a glass for everyone. And right in the middle of the table was a big plate of those chocolate chip cookies. Her mother put one on Sarah's wheelchair tray.

"Can she eat all right?" Sue asked.

Sarah's mother paused with the plate of cookies in one hand and looked at Sue. "Ask *her*," she said.

"Of course she can," Amy answered Sue.

"Let *her* show you," her mother insisted.

No one spoke for a while after that. Sarah wished Sue wasn't there. She drank apple juice through a long straw and bit into her cookie. It didn't taste as good as she had thought it would.

When they had finished eating, Sue said it was time for her to go home, and Amy offered to walk her down to the corner. Sarah and her mother sat alone at the table.

"Don't mind Sue," her mother told Sarah. "She just couldn't think what to say."

Sarah chewed on another cookie, slowly, hardly tasting it. It seemed that people who could talk still didn't always know what to say. And they didn't know how to speak to people like her. They had this wonderful gift of spoken words, and sometimes they used it in ways that hurt other people.

"I love you, Kitten," her mother said and gave her a

quick hug. "Remember when I used to hold you on my lap and sing lullabies? You're too big now."

"Too big now," Sarah said in symbols, and she meant not just that she seemed bigger and heavier, but that she felt more grown up inside. And then, while her mother watched her board, she pointed first to her mother's picture in the row of photographs of family and friends, and then to symbols:

love you, too

When Amy came back, her mother had words for her. "Look, Amy," she said, "you ought to be careful how you talk about Sarah when your friends are here. They may not know she can hear, but *you* know. She wants you to talk *to* her, not *about* her. You do it, and they'll get the idea."

Amy shrugged. "Maybe I shouldn't bring anyone home."

"That's not fair. Sarah needs to get to know other people, too."

Sarah banged on her wheelchair tray with her good left hand. They were doing just what her mother had said not to do, talking about her as if she couldn't hear or weren't even there.

They didn't pay any attention, so she banged again.

"Oh, that Sarah!" Amy was saying, and she made a face. Sarah just sat still.

"Look, Amy," her mother said, "it *is* hard. But we all have to help."

"I *do* help, Mama," Amy protested. "I help all I can."

"I know you do. You've been wonderful. Perhaps I'm asking too much of you."

The front door slammed. Sarah's father was home early.

"Hi, Poppa!" Amy called, and she ran to him.

Sarah pushed her switch again to start her wheelchair going.

"Hello, Father!" she wanted to say, and she pointed at symbols. But he wasn't near enough to see, and she would never get to him as fast as Amy.

2

She Ought to See
More of the World

The next morning, Sarah woke early and opened her eyes. In the dim light, she looked around at the familiar things that meant home to her. White ruffled curtains stirred in the breeze at the open window. A yellow cloth duck her Aunt Laura had made for her years ago sat on the shelf. Beside it were her books; she knew them, even across the room, by their shapes and colors. Her mother used to read these to her. Now she could read them herself.

On another shelf sat Sarah's portable tape player—her "boom box." She remembered how Amy had looked and looked in different stores until she found one Sarah could hold and work with one hand at the same time. And it was small enough to fit in beside her on the wheelchair. There was a pile of tapes beside the player, all without their cases, because that was easier for Sarah. Amy had thought of that, too.

Sarah's clothes for the day had been laid across the back of a chair—underpants, her favorite jeans, a red T-shirt, and red socks to match. Beyond the chair was the white door that led to the hall, shadowy in the early light, from where her mother would come to get her ready for the day.

She closed her eyes and just listened. Earlier in the summer, robins had raised a family in the tree outside her window. Some of them still slept there. Their waking pattern always repeated itself: A lazy peep; a pause; then another peep, and another. And at last a real birdsong. Over and over, the same things happened in the world. Birds and animals and people were born, and their mothers took care of them. Birds grew up quickly and made more baby birds. People were much slower; they needed their mothers longer, but then they had time to discover who they really were.

She opened her eyes again and looked straight up. It was brighter now. Sunlight and leaf shadows made dancing patterns on the ceiling. And again came that birdsong, somewhere in the whispering leaves.

She had to go to the bathroom. *That* was enough to

take her out of a daydream. There had been a time when she would try to get out of bed herself. *Push*, she would tell herself, *move that leg, lift yourself. Push.* Mrs. Brady would try to get her to do that when she came to do exercises with her. It had never worked. Yet it had been a long time before she could give up hoping that someday, by some sort of magic that would come in the night, she might be able to walk.

She *had* to go to the bathroom.

"Mama!" she tried to call, and of course, "Agghh" came out instead of words. Her mother appeared in the doorway, dressed in a long blue nightgown.

"Hush, dear, I came as soon as I could."

Sarah cried out with all the voice she had. But then she was held close against her mother, and warmth and comfort chased away the anger.

"All right, Kitten," her mother said. Gently, she let Sarah fall back onto the bed. The wheelchair stood against one wall, with its batteries plugged into an electric outlet for recharging overnight. Sarah's mother unplugged it and moved it close to the bed. Then, grasping Sarah tight around the middle, with a quick twist she heaved her into it.

Down the hall to the bathroom. Sarah's mother pushed the wheelchair next to the toilet, slid Sarah onto it, and supported her back with one arm.

"There now," she said.

Another day was starting for Sarah.

Sarah's mother quickly pushed Sarah's arms into the sleeves of a pink robe that had been hanging on the back of the bathroom door, wrapped it around her, and fastened the wide strap that held Sarah upright against the back of the wheelchair. Then she hurried to get herself dressed and make her way down the hall to the kitchen. Breakfast was a busy time.

Sarah, meanwhile, wheeled herself close to the bathroom sink and washed her face with her good left hand. She pulled a comb out of the bag that hung from the arm of her wheelchair and ran it quickly through her hair. Her mother had put a mirror on the wall, at sitting level. Sarah looked. Brown eyes, plain, round face. And her hair—brown curls sticking out every which way. She tried again with the comb. Another look—better. That would have to do.

When she reached the dining area, the rest of the family was already settled for breakfast. Her father peered at her over the newspaper he was reading, but he did not say anything. Amy was bent over a hot cup of cocoa, blowing on it. Her dark, straight hair nearly hid the cup.

"Hiya, Squib!" she called out cheerfully, as she tossed her hair back.

Sarah waved at Amy, appreciating the love that came with being called Squib.

"Soft-boiled egg, anybody?" their mother asked.

"No time, Ma," Amy said.

Her father spoke for the first time. "Why don't you help your mother with breakfast?"

Amy mumbled into her cocoa, "In a hurry, got that Girl Scout trip."

I'd help if I could, Sarah was thinking. *Mama, I want to help.* Her mother had put her breakfast tray over her symbols and she couldn't say anything, so she just made noises and waved her hand.

"I know you're hungry," her mother said, and she put a glass of orange juice on Sarah's tray. It fitted into a round, indented place where it couldn't slide off. Sarah drank it with a long straw fastened to the edge of the glass.

She *was* hungry, but that wasn't what she had wanted to say. The words were all there in her head, but she couldn't say them. She looked at those people, her family, talking about soft-boiled eggs and Girl Scout trips. Words spilled out of their mouths so easily; they did not even know how marvelous this was. To

27

Sarah it was magic. As long as she lived, it would seem to her the most astonishing magic in the world.

"Bye," Amy called from the doorway as she rushed off.

The three remaining Bennetts had their boiled eggs and toast. Sarah ate slowly, carefully, with her good hand. Her mother had cracked Sarah's egg and emptied it into a little bowl with rubber on the bottom to keep it from slipping. Sarah's spoon had a bent handle that made it easier for her to reach both the food and her mouth. She daydreamed, while she ate, of Amy with a busload of laughing girls going out of the city, into meadows bright with flowers.

She wanted to speak to her mother, who was busy talking and drinking coffee with her father. Sarah tried pointing at her mouth, but no one looked. All right, she would ring her bell. Her mother had fastened this bell to the back of her wheelchair, and Sarah could ring it by pulling a string. Now she pulled hard. R-r-ring! No one seemed to hear. She pulled the string again.

"Stop ringing that bell!" her father yelled.

"She wants to say something, Tom!" her mother said. "How else can she tell us?"

She set the coffeepot down on the table and lifted Sarah's breakfast tray so they could see the symbols.

"*I wish I could go,*" Sarah said with her symbols.

"Where, Kitten?"

"*With Amy.*" Sarah pointed to her sister's picture on the board.

"I know, Kitten. You hardly ever go anywhere."

Sarah's mother put more toast in the toaster, slowly, as if she were thinking of something else.

"Tom," she said to her husband, "we've got to take Sarah on longer trips. She ought to be seeing more of the world."

"You know how hard it is, Liz, even if we take Sarah's old wheelchair. Someone has to lift Sarah onto the car seat and fasten her strap. Then the wheelchair gets folded up and put into the trunk of the car, and someone hauls it out after we get there. That's a lot of work, though that wheelchair *is* lighter than the electric one. Besides, *Sarah's* heavier now, and I can't always go with you."

Sarah couldn't think of any way to make this easier. She sighed.

"Well, there must be *some* way," her mother said.

"Such as what?" Her father snorted.

"Maybe we could get a van. We could put the whole wheelchair in, with Sarah in it, and the rest of us could sit up front. I've thought about this a lot, Tom."

"Liz, do you know what a van *costs*?"

"A second-hand one, then. Maybe I could earn some money tutoring school kids, or something like that."

"Be realistic, Liz. You're busy enough already."

"Well, I don't want Sarah sitting around with nothing to do all summer."

Sarah's father looked at his wife over his coffee cup and grinned. "You don't give up, do you, Liz?"

She laughed. "You know *me*, Tom."

"Okay, I'll see what I can do."

Sarah chortled with relief. That was just like her father. He could get terribly mad about something, and a few minutes later he'd change his mind. He was like that with her. Most of the time he hardly talked to her, and she didn't even know if he cared. Then he'd come across with something wonderful and expensive, like the electric wheelchair. He'd given it to her as a surprise on her eighth birthday. Before that, she couldn't go anywhere by herself, not even across a room in her own house. Someone had to push her wheelchair.

Maybe some other people were like her father; they could show their love only by giving gifts. She'd rather have the steady love her mother gave, through all the ordinary happenings of every day.

"Got to go now," her father said, and soon he was on

his way down the street to take the bus to work.

"More toast?" Sarah's mother asked absent-mind-edly. Sarah pointed to "OK," at the top of her board.

"Your father will do something, just wait and see," her mother said. "Don't mind his getting upset. He works hard making money for us, selling insurance all day, and we need so many things."

Sarah nodded. She knew her father worked hard; he had told her that himself. But—how could she become part of the world if she hardly ever went anywhere? What was her father going to do about that?

3

Love and Brownies

After breakfast, Sarah's mother dressed her carefully, making sure nothing pinched or hurt. Sarah helped with her good hand whenever she could, pulling up her pants, smoothing down her T-shirt. Every day her mother did this, every day with love, ending always with a hug.

"Now," her mother said, "I've got to clean up in the kitchen. I'll get your book—that will keep you busy."

Sarah propelled herself into the living room, to the picture window where she loved to look out. Her mother brought Sarah's copy of *Tuck Everlasting*. She set it up on a stand that held the pages open, but not so tightly that Sarah couldn't turn them.

Sarah loved the people in *Tuck Everlasting*, but she didn't feel like reading this morning. It might be fun to watch television, but the Bennett television set was in the family room, down in the basement. There was no way to get the wheelchair down those stairs with Sarah in it. She could watch television only when someone carried her and strapped her into a special chair down there. It was hard for her mother to do that; Sarah knew she was too heavy now. Her father carried her down, now and then. Sarah loved watching the news, just like a grownup.

"Why is our TV down there?" Amy had asked one day last year.

"I don't want you or Sarah watching it all day," her mother had said.

Well anyway, right now Sarah wanted to think about her new school. It would be very different from the old one—so many more children, most of them walking with their own two legs. And maybe nobody else with Blissymbols. But she belonged in this new school, too! She had been disappointed when she was told she would not be in a regular class. Instead, hers would be a class with just a few children, all of them with some sort of learning problem. *Learning isn't my problem*, she had protested.

"What would they do with you in a regular class, Squib?" Amy had commented. "You couldn't expect the teacher to teach twenty-five kids and pay attention to your symbols, besides."

Well, at least she'd be in a regular *school,* and maybe someday she could attend one class with those twenty-five kids.

It was scary, thinking about doing something so different. Quick, another daydream. She was off on a trip with her imaginary friend, Margaret. Sarah had never met a Margaret, but this one was real enough to her and as timeless as the Tuck family in her book. Unlike the Tucks, however, Margaret lived in a wheelchair, as Sarah did. But she could talk. In fact—and this was the most wonderful thing of all—when Sarah went on trips with Margaret, *she* could talk, too. Side by side in their wheelchairs, they went right out of the house, down the ramp that covered the front steps, and up to the woods at the end of the street.

Sarah knew these woods. Amy had taken her there in the springtime, saying, "You ought to go *some*where, Squib!" She had picked two spring flowers with pink-striped petals and handed them to Sarah. "Hold the stems tight," she had said, and Sarah had, all the way home.

There were paths in the woods, but not for wheelchairs. Sarah and the imaginary Margaret sat at the edge of the woods a little while, as if waiting for something to happen. And then it *did* happen. Margaret reached out a hand to Sarah, and they both stood up, right in front of their wheelchairs. Hand in hand, they walked down a path into the woods. Amy had told Sarah how soft the earth felt under her feet in the woods. Now she could feel it herself. Birds sang. Branches moved in the wind.

Sarah and Margaret called to the animals they thought must live in the woods. They had done this before. Sarah wanted a bear, not a scary one, just a teddy bear named Willie, like the one her mother had given her last Christmas. Margaret called to a rabbit. Peter, of course. That didn't work today. No animals came.

"I want a friend," Sarah complained.

"I am your friend," Margaret said.

"I need a *real* friend," Sarah replied.

She wondered suddenly if she would be able to get animals to visit her this way anymore. Maybe she would even have to say good-bye to Margaret.

"I need a real *friend,"* she told herself again.

She looked out the window. That was where the real world was, somewhere out there, and it was going to be *her* world.

A tall woman wearing a pink sweater waved as she went by. She was Ruth Burroughs, who lived in the next house up the street. Sarah had had many conversations with Ruth Burroughs in the garden behind the house. Surely *she* was a friend. But Sarah needed someone near her own age, too. All the children in her class at Ingleside, her special school, had been her friends. She was not sure she would ever see them again. They lived too far away, scattered all over the city. She sighed.

Sarah moved into the kitchen, her favorite room. When she had first brought symbols home from school, her mother had decorated the kitchen walls with them, so they could practice together. Her mother had printed the word for each symbol, just as on Sarah's board. That was so people who had not learned the symbols would know what was being said.

Some of the symbols Sarah's mother had put up were still there:

mother	father	sister	happy	angry

chair	thirsty	hello	good-bye

Cooking with her mother was the most fun for Sarah, especially when they made cookies or brownies. That afternoon it was brownies. Sarah measured the flour by spooning it, a little at a time, from a big canister into a measuring cup. Then she poured it into a bowl. Sugar came next; then a little baking powder. It took time to get all this just right, but Sarah's mother never made her hurry.

Meanwhile, her mother had been melting butter and squares of chocolate on the stove. She put them in another bowl, cracked an egg into it, and let Sarah mix everything together. Sarah stirred and stirred with a big spoon, using her whole arm. But where were the nuts? She stopped long enough to point to *nut* on her board:

seed + tree

"Of course, nuts!" her mother said. "I almost forgot." She poured in the chopped nuts from a bowl on the counter and Sarah stirred again. "These really are *your* brownies," Sarah's mother said, as she poured the batter into a pan. She put it in the oven, and set the timer at a half hour. Sarah and her mother exchanged smiles of satisfaction.

This was a good time to talk. Sarah wanted her mother to tell her, over and over again, what happened when she was a baby and why she couldn't walk or talk. Even though she already knew most of the story, talking about it helped her to understand.

Her mother had explained that part of Sarah's brain may have been injured, either about the time she was born, or before. Or, her brain had failed to develop as it should. It was hard for doctors to know just what had happened. Whatever the cause, it meant that Sarah's brain could not send the right signals to most of her muscles, and they could not move properly. That included the muscles she would need for talking.

Sarah had the spastic kind of cerebral palsy; the type you had depended on the part of the brain that was affected.

"Many people with cerebral palsy can walk pretty well," Sarah's mother had told her. "Most can talk, though not always clearly." *Lucky people*, Sarah thought.

"Tell me again about when I was a baby," Sarah was saying now.

Her mother nodded, as if she knew Sarah would want that. "You were a lovely baby, even though you couldn't move around like most babies."

"That doctor—" Sarah said with her symbols.

"Yes, that doctor who told me you had cerebral palsy. When he found out you couldn't speak, he told me you would never learn much."

"Dumb doctor," Sarah wanted to say. No symbol for that kind of "dumb." She spelled it out with the letters at the top of her board. It came out *"dum."* Sarah laughed.

"Well, you know, Sarah," her mother went on, "when a person can't say anything it's easy for people, even doctors, to think they aren't very smart. And it's true that *some* cerebral palsied children aren't bright; of course, some otherwise normal people aren't very bright, either."

"And me?"

"You seemed pretty smart to *us*, but we weren't sure what you could do. We wanted you to have every chance in the world, even if you couldn't speak."

"And look, Mama!" Sarah pointed. *"I can say almost anything I want, with symbols."*

"Yes, you had the words in your head all the time."

Sarah's mother gave her a hug.

The bell on the timer rang.

"Brownies!" her mother said. She opened the oven door, and there they were. "Mm-mm-mm," she said, pulling the brownies out of the oven. Sarah tried to say "Mm-mm," too, as she sniffed the wonderful, hot aroma of chocolate.

Her mother poked the brown dough with one finger and drew it back fast. "Hot! We'll have to let them cool. Come on, I'll take you to the bathroom."

They were eating brownies together and laughing when Amy came home from her trip.

"Better than ever, Kitten," Sarah's mother was saying to Sarah.

"Agghh," Sarah said, as she stuffed a piece of brownie into her mouth. Her mother held up another piece.

"More?" she asked.

"Un-uh," Sarah said, meaning *no,* because her mouth was already full. Her mother made a funny face, and they both laughed and laughed.

Neither of them noticed that the back door had slammed and Amy was there.

"Guess what happened, Ma!" Amy exclaimed.

No one answered. Sarah and her mother were much too busy laughing. Suddenly, Sarah saw Amy grab the brownie from her mother's hand and throw it on the floor. Then, so fast that no one knew what was happening, Amy slapped Sarah's face.

Sarah looked at Amy with astonishment and started to cry.

Amy turned on her mother. "You're always doing nice things with her!" she raged. "You never have time for me!"

"That's not true, Amy," her mother protested.

"It is! It's Sarah, Sarah all the time! What about me?"

She stamped out of the room. There was silence for a moment, and then her mother followed her.

Sarah stopped crying. Why was Amy so mad at her? She tried to bring back Margaret so they could get away together and forget all this trouble, but Margaret would not come.

There was a crumb of brownie on her wheelchair tray. Sarah picked it up, put it in her mouth, and chewed it slowly. It didn't taste good anymore.

It was suppertime before Sarah saw Amy again. Amy did not talk to her. She seemed to feel better, though; she told her father about playing baseball at Chase's Park, where she had gone on the Girl Scout trip.

When Sarah's mother put her to bed, she sat on the bed and stroked Sarah's forehead. "It *is* hard for Amy sometimes, you know," she said. "You need a lot more things done for you than she does. That's lucky for her, but she doesn't always see it that way."

Sarah nodded. She wanted to ask if Amy was still her friend, but she did not have her symbol board. Her mother was quiet a while, just looking at Sarah. Then she kissed her on the same cheek that had been slapped by Amy and went out, leaving the door open a little.

Sarah lay there listening to voices in the rest of the house and watching the faint stream of light that came through the crack in the doorway. Suddenly it got wider, and the door opened. Amy came in, carrying something in each hand.

"Look, Squib," she said. "I brought you some cocoa and a brownie. Remember how I used to do that when you were little?"

Sarah remembered. It had been a long time since Amy had done this for her.

Amy set the cocoa and brownie down on the table beside Sarah's bed, arranged Sarah's pillows, and pulled her up into a sitting position. She hadn't forgotten to bring a straw, and she held the cocoa so Sarah could drink it. Sarah made happy noises in appreciation.

"I'm sorry about hitting you," Amy said. "You're still my Sarah-Squib, aren't you?"

Sarah nodded her head—*yes, oh yes*. She drank the

cocoa all the way to the bottom. Amy broke the brownie in half and handed her a piece.

"Remember Sue?" she said. "She told me the funniest joke today. Want to hear it?"

Another nod—*yes, yes* again.

"It's a riddle," Amy said. "What do you call fifty rabbits standing in a row, all hopping backwards? You're supposed to say you don't know, and then I give you the answer: A receding hairline!"

Amy was roaring with laughter, and Sarah joined in. Such a good joke. Sarah laughed so hard she nearly choked on her brownie. Amy held her by the shoulders and patted her back while they laughed together.

When they had stopped laughing, Sarah picked up a crumb of brownie from the bedspread and put it in her mouth. It was delicious. She was full of love for this sister who brought her cocoa and brownies and shared with her such wonderful jokes.

4

Wheels!

There was Aunt Laura. She was the younger sister of Sarah's mother, but she was not like her mother at all. Her mother was a "real homebody"—that was what her father said. Not Aunt Laura. She was a lawyer. Sarah was not sure what lawyers did, but she knew that Aunt Laura's job kept her away from home all day and sometimes half the night. Weekends were different; then Aunt Laura would often be off at some country resort—swimming in summer, skiing in winter. Vacations meant cruises. "You meet the most marvelous men on those boats," she would say. Sarah could never keep track of them—Sam, Charlie, Andrew—a different man each time.

Aunt Laura talked constantly about her vacations, the theater, and parties.

"She has so much fun," Sarah's mother sometimes said. Perhaps, Sarah thought, her mother wished *she* could have that kind of fun. Not much chance, with a family to cook for, the house to keep clean, and a daughter stuck in a wheelchair, needing her all the time.

Aunt Laura always came with a big box of Danish pastries, or a cake with sticky frosting, or a bottle of wine, "for the *big* children," she would say. She was slim and wore clothes that made her look pretty—neat suits, and blouses with ruffles at the neck. Her high-heeled shoes made clicking sounds on the kitchen floor. Sarah's mother's shoes were low-heeled with rubber soles, so Sarah couldn't even hear when she was coming.

Sarah wasn't sure how she felt about Aunt Laura. Her aunt didn't seem to be someone you could depend on, like her mother. And yet, Sarah was fascinated by Aunt Laura, too. Aunt Laura belonged to the wide world outside, where she was sure there was excitement and pleasure such as she could not even imagine.

Sometimes, on a Saturday, Aunt Laura would take care of Sarah when her parents and Amy all had to go places. Sarah wished her mother wouldn't leave her alone with Aunt Laura. Of course, Sarah was used to having a sitter in the evening, now and then, when her mother and father wanted to go out. Ruth Burroughs might come, or Mrs. Taylor, who lived down the street. Sarah's mother would put her to bed early and then Sarah might play a game with Amy or Ruth or Mrs. Taylor. All the sitter had to do after that was sit.

Daytimes, now that she was older, Sarah could stay with Amy. But there might be Aunt Laura on a Saturday, and that could make problems. For one thing, at first Aunt Laura had refused to take Sarah's symbols seriously.

"What's this?" she had exclaimed when she first saw Sarah's symbol board. "A new game?"

"Symbols," Amy explained. "Sarah can talk with them."

"Well, not really," Aunt Laura drawled.

"She can," Amy insisted. "Just look, Aunt Laura."

Aunt Laura looked. "I can't be bothered learning all that," she said.

It had been hard to persuade her that she didn't have to learn very many symbols. At last, when she was taking care of Sarah, Aunt Laura would let her say she was hungry or thirsty or needed to go to the bathroom. Not much else.

"Sarah can talk with you better if you learn more of the symbols," Sarah's mother explained.

47

"That stuff really isn't for me," Aunt Laura said. "We got along all right before."

We didn't, Sarah wanted to say. Something often went wrong when Aunt Laura took over.

"She can feed herself," Sarah's mother would say when Aunt Laura was to give her lunch. "Don't do it for her."

Sarah could see, though, that Aunt Laura would *rather* do it for her. She got upset when Sarah's milk dribbled down her chin; Aunt Laura would wipe it away, hard, with a napkin. And once, she got really mad when Sarah was trying to balance a piece of fishcake on her spoon and it bounced off onto the floor and slid under the table.

"What a mess!" Aunt Laura exclaimed, as she picked up the piece of fishcake and threw it in the garbage. "I don't see how your mother stands it."

Sarah tried to hold back the tears, but she couldn't. They poured down her cheeks, and she made little crying sounds behind her clenched teeth.

"Oh, all right, Sarah," Aunt Laura said. "I know you can't help it."

She kept wiping Sarah's tears until Sarah reached up with her good hand and pushed Aunt Laura's arm away. *Let me alone*, Sarah wanted to say, *just let me alone*.

Sometimes, though, Aunt Laura would talk to her about her travels. Sarah would sit entranced, her head a jumble of palm trees, sandy beaches, and dancing in the moonlight with that special man.

Aunt Laura came over one evening with her color slides of the West Indies and nearby islands, and a slide projector.

"Sarah wants to see where I went," she said, though Sarah had never been able to get such a message across to Aunt Laura.

Sarah had seen pictures of palm trees and beaches in books, and her class in school had learned something about the West Indies. But now, as colorful scene after scene appeared on the screen, all this seemed much more real. And look! There was Aunt Laura herself in the group of people on a sunny beach that was dotted with striped umbrellas.

"Aruba," Aunt Laura was saying, "that was the best trip of all. How d'you like my bathing suit, Sarah?"

Aunt Laura's bathing suit was tight and striped green and pink, like the nearby umbrellas. Sarah herself had a pink bathing suit she had worn when her class did exercises in the swimming pool at school. But it was nothing like Aunt Laura's.

Everyone is so happy in Aunt Laura's slides, Sarah

observed to herself. *No one needs a wheelchair.*

"You know, Sarah," Aunt Laura said one Saturday (after she had burned the hamburger, but Sarah ate it anyway), "they ought to take you on a trip somewhere. All you do is sit around and maybe go out in the garden once in a while."

That wasn't *quite* all. But Sarah nodded at Aunt Laura and pointed at YES in the corner of her symbol board. And then at the symbol for *sad*—but Aunt Laura wasn't looking.

"You'd feel like a new person," Aunt Laura went on. "Everybody needs to travel. Can't your father do something?"

Yes, oh yes. When was her father going to get that van?

Five days later Sarah's father phoned from his office to say he'd be home a little late and he had a big surprise for everyone.

At seven o'clock a blue van drove up to the house.

"What's *that?*" Amy wanted to know.

Sarah was sitting at the living room window, and she saw the van. She knew right away what it was, a car big enough to get the wheelchair into, for *her.* Her father had done it!

"What's *that?*" Amy said again.

The van was bulky looking and obviously not new. The fenders were rusting, and paint had been scratched off the sides in several places.

"Well, here it is!" their father said as he opened the front door. "A car for Sarah and her wheelchair."

Their mother came out of the kitchen when she heard that. "Let's *see*, Tom!"

"Well, anyway, now we have two cars," Amy said.

"We won't have two," her father explained. "We'll have to sell the Chevy."

"You mean we'll just have *that?*"

"Just that, and I was lucky to find it."

"What are my friends going to say?" Amy wailed. "Sue's family has two *real* cars."

"I don't care what they say," her father said. "We're doing the best we can for Sarah."

"Oh yes, for Sarah, we have to have that wrecky looking old car for Sarah."

"Stop it, Amy," her mother scolded. "You know better than that."

Sulking, Amy went into her room and closed the door. Sarah looked out the window at the van, trying to see what there was about it that got Amy so upset. Maybe it wasn't pretty, but to Sarah it looked just wonderful. It was her way out into the world; nothing Amy

51

said or did could change that.

The next day was Saturday. Sarah's father went to the lumberyard in the morning and came back with four lengths of board a foot wide. Harry Burroughs, Ruth's husband, came over from next door to help him carry the boards into the basement. After that, Sarah could hear noises down there that sounded like some kind of pounding and grinding.

"They're making a ramp for the van," her mother told her. "So we can get your wheelchair in."

Sarah raised her left hand and put it behind her ear. That was one way of asking about sounds.

"Sawing boards and hammering nails," her mother said. "And you know what? They're going to make a ramp for the back steps, too."

That would make a difference. Sarah banged her hand onto her wheelchair tray, meaning "Hurray!" Until now, whenever she went to the garden in back of the house, she had to go down the ramp in the front and around the side of the house on a bumpy cement walk.

The sawing and hammering continued. Aunt Laura arrived in her red Colt, pulling to a sudden stop behind the van. She was going out to lunch and a new play at the theater with Sarah's mother.

Aunt Laura seemed to share Amy's feelings about the van.

"Couldn't you get something better looking?" she asked Sarah's father as he emerged from the basement.

"No, I couldn't," he told her. "I'm not made of money, you know."

"I thought you were going to the ball game," Aunt Laura said.

He shook his head. "We're making a ramp for the van. That's more important."

"Well, I never thought I'd see the day—something more important to you than a ball game."

Sarah's father didn't answer that. Harry Burroughs came up the cellar stairs just then, and he and Sarah's father went to the Burroughs house for lunch. Sarah wished she could go, too, but there was no way she could get into that house.

Today she was to have lunch with Amy. Her mother and Aunt Laura departed with a flurry of good-byes. Sarah sat waiting in the dining area. That van. Already, in imagination, she was being driven away from home, beyond the city, to meadows bright with flowers. She had seen pictures of meadows like that, but never a real one. Of course, she had gone to school in a van, with an elevator that lifted her inside, wheelchair and all. But the daily trip had always been the same, through city streets, as they picked up five other children, each in a wheelchair.

Where was Amy? Maybe she was so angry about the van that she didn't want to fix lunch for her. But then Amy appeared as if out of nowhere.

"About that van—" she began.

Sarah's heart sank. *"I need it,"* she said with her symbol board.

"I know, Squib," Amy assured her. "And it's not your fault it isn't pretty. I won't fuss about it anymore."

"Good."

"Hungry?"

Sarah nodded.

"Mama left some chicken soup. I'll make peanut butter sandwiches. Applesauce for dessert."

Lunch with Amy was always fun. She could heat up the soup and talk at the same time, just like their mother, and she never forgot to see what Sarah wanted to say. This time, of course, their conversation started with the van.

"Think of all the places you'll be going, Squib!" Amy said.

And Sarah: *"I want to see the world."*

"That's a tall order, but you'll be seeing more of it

than you ever did before."

"*Poppa gives me things,*" Sarah said.

"He sure does—the wheelchair, and now this!"

"*Does he love me?*"

"Of course. He loves all of us."

"*Not like Mama.*"

Amy was silent for a moment. "No, not like Mama. No one will ever love you like Mama."

"*She loves you, too.*"

"Yes, but you're kind of special to her, Squib."

"*Does that upset you?*"

"Sometimes."

"*I'm sorry.*"

Amy gave her a hug. "That's not your fault either, Squib."

Sarah laughed and took a big bite of her peanut butter sandwich.

After lunch, Amy said she had to call Sue, and that took a long time. Sarah watched the clock: ten minutes, fifteen, twenty. She was bored.

Sunlight flickered on the leaves outside the kitchen window. A bird sang in the garden. That was where she wanted to be. She wheeled herself to the front door; it was partly open. She managed to swing it wide with her good arm. The screen door, she knew, could be opened by just bumping into it.

Down the ramp she went, then paused in the shade of the big maple tree in front. Around to the side, bump, bump, and finally into the back yard. There was not much blooming in the garden now—a few early asters and big pink blossoms on the rose-of-Sharon bush by the back steps. *They're like hollyhocks, only on a bush,* Sarah thought.

They had finished lunch next door. Sarah knew because Ruth was busy in her garden. Sarah could see Ruth's blond head bobbing up and down as she worked. There was an occasional clink of tool against stone. Then Ruth was singing, something about an answer "blowing in the wind." Sarah wondered if Ruth Burroughs had any special answers for the troubles people had.

"Hello, Sarah," Ruth said as she peered over the fence. "Look at this earth." She held out a handful of garden soil. "Good brown earth, that's what makes the garden grow." She rubbed some of it between her fingers.

"Here!" she said, and without further explanation she strode around the end of the fence and into the Bennetts' yard. "Feel it yourself, Sarah."

Sarah put her hand out, wondering if she wanted to

feel that brown stuff. Ruth put some in her good hand. Sarah rubbed it awkwardly between her fingers; it felt rough and warm. Then she looked straight up into Ruth Burroughs' eyes; she had forgotten how blue they were. There were no words for this blue.

Finally Ruth said, "Earth feels good, doesn't it, Sarah?"

"*Yes. Thank you. Yes,*" Sarah wanted to say, but she could not point with her hand holding that dirt. Those were somehow not the right words, anyway. Sometimes they would not come, either in her head or on the symbol board.

Ruth Burroughs seemed to know what Sarah was thinking. "People don't always need words—you know that, Sarah? Lots of things can be shared without any words at all." And she gave Sarah a gentle kiss on the forehead.

Sarah stared gratefully at this loving neighbor who said you didn't always need words. Then she poured the brown earth slowly out of her hand onto the ground, still feeling its warmth.

"Earth to earth," Ruth said, and they were both still for a while. The only sound in the garden was a hum of bees.

Then, "You know, Sarah," Ruth said, "I saw the most

wonderful garden the other day. It was on top of a brick wall, just the right height for a wheelchair, so people like you could dig in the earth and grow flowers."

Growing flowers? People in wheelchairs, like herself? Marvelous. But who were these people? The only people like herself she'd ever known were the children in her special school.

"Sarah," Ruth went on, "now that you have that van, perhaps we can go there. I'd been hoping, anyway, that we could get you there to meet Johnnie."

She paused, looking to see if Sarah had anything to say. She could read the symbols almost as well as Sarah's mother.

"Who?"

"You know, Johnnie, my nephew. He's in a wheelchair, like you, because he has cerebral palsy, too. But he can talk. Sarah, you'd like Johnnie."

"He has this garden at his house?"

"No. He lives in an institution, a very big house called Plainview, with other children. Some of them are teenagers, like Johnnie—he's fourteen."

"Why do they live there?"

"Well, they all have some kind of disability—they need special help, the way you do."

Sarah turned this over in her mind. An institution,

where lots of children lived together so they could get help. She had heard of such places, but she didn't know much about them.

"Who helps them?"

"Oh, house mothers, nurses, everybody. And they help each other."

Sarah felt shivery inside. This didn't sound much like having a home.

"Where is J's mother?" (J for Johnnie.)

"She has a job, even some weekends, so she can't take care of him. His father went away. Sarah, it's a *nice* place. Johnnie's all right there. His mother comes twice a week."

Now Sarah felt really shivery. Imagine seeing your own mother only twice a week! Nobody in that place had their own family there.

"No," she said. *"I don't want to go there."*

"Please, Sarah, you don't *know*. Let's go there and see. Johnnie does get lonely sometimes, and he'll like you—you're a sweet girl."

Lonely? With all those people around?

In spite of herself, though, Sarah was curious. She was lonely, too, and maybe Johnnie would be her friend. He was in a wheelchair; she wondered if he could move his legs at all, or his arms.

"*Maybe,*" she said. And then, "*They all have gardens?*"

"Those that can dig. The walls for the gardens were built just this summer. Johnnie put petunias in his."

A place where people in wheelchairs could plant gardens. That would be something to see. If she decided to go at all.

5

The Awful Outing

It would be some time before Sarah would get to visit Johnnie at Plainview. Her father insisted that he should go along on the first few trips in the van, and no one could persuade him to go to Plainview.

"I don't need to see any more disabled kids," he said.

The first trip in the van was to be to the zoo, on a Saturday. The whole family would go—Aunt Laura, too.

"You'll see real bears at the zoo, Squib," Amy had told her, "and lions with big shaggy manes, and monkeys. Sometimes the monkeys look at you as if they were people."

The wonder of it! Sarah had hardly known any animals at all. Her teddy bear, Willie, after all, was not real.

One afternoon, Amy had come home carrying a black, purring ball of fur and set it down gently in Sarah's lap.

"Sue's cat had kittens a while ago, and now they're giving them away," Amy said. "Maybe Mama will let us keep this one."

Sarah had never known anything so soft and warm. She stroked the kitten with her left hand and tried to purr along with it: "Ah-h-h. . ."

A real live animal to hold and love.

But when their father came home and saw the kitten, he said to Amy, "Look! You can take that animal right back to Sue's. Your mother has enough work to do without looking after a kitten you won't take care of."

Amy knew better than to argue with her father when he spoke in that stern tone of voice. She picked up the kitten and walked out of the house and along the street with tears pouring down her face.

Sarah sat in her wheelchair just whimpering a little, not wanting her father to hear.

"*Other* kids have cats and dogs," Amy complained to Sarah when she got back from Sue's. "We don't even have goldfish."

"*It's because of me,*" Sarah said. "*Mama has to work so much for me.*"

"Oh, *Sarah*," Amy said. "Don't go thinking *this* is your fault. It's the way our father is, that's all."

They were both silent, and after a while Sarah could see a smile beginning on Amy's face.

"Anyway, Squib," she said, "when you and I are grown up we'll have all the kittens we want."

Being grown up was not something Sarah had thought much about. She wasn't going to start now. Instead, she contemplated the zoo, where she would see all those animals Amy had told her about. Think of seeing lions! She wondered if the lions in the zoo would look as fierce as the ones she had seen in a book about Africa that Amy had brought home from school.

There had been considerable discussion about whether the zoo was the right place to take Sarah.

"Kids always love the zoo," her father had said.

"I know," her mother commented. "But it's going to be crowded on Saturday, and Sarah isn't used to being with all those people. She'll get confused. And besides, people may ask funny questions."

"Come on, Liz, she'll eat it up," her father insisted.

"Well, perhaps if we don't stay too long." Sarah's mother had sighed as she put a dish of applesauce on Sarah's wheelchair tray.

No one asked Sarah if she wanted to go, but of

course she did. The zoo was fine, but she would be happy to go almost anywhere.

Amy had phoned Aunt Laura. Would she come?

"Sure, baby, I'd love to," Aunt Laura said. "But not in that van, you won't have room. I'll drive myself and meet you there."

Now the day had arrived. Sarah woke up tingling all over with anticipation. Getting dressed couldn't happen fast enough.

Breakfast seemed to take forever that morning. Sarah was so flustered that her fried egg flew off her tray and somehow landed on Amy's plate, and her toast ended up jam side down on the floor.

"Good for you, Squib!" Amy said. "I bet I couldn't do that with an egg!"

She put the egg back on Sarah's plate. Her mother put another piece of bread in the toaster.

It was ten o'clock before they were ready to put Sarah and her wheelchair in the van. The day was already hot under the summer sun. They were to meet Aunt Laura at the zoo at half-past ten.

First, her mother strapped her tight against the back of the wheelchair. "So we won't lose you," she said.

The back doors of the van were opened, and the ramp was set up.

"I'd better push you in this time, Sarah," her father said, and he started pushing the wheelchair, front first, up the ramp.

"Not that way!" her mother exclaimed.

"Why not?"

"She won't be able to see out; the only windows are at the back."

Sarah looked. Sure enough, there were no windows on the sides of the van.

"Oh," her father said, and he turned the wheelchair around. "Up you go backwards, then!"

He grabbed the arms of the wheelchair and pushed Sarah backwards into the van. Then he fastened her brake and clipped onto each arm of the wheelchair special straps he had attached to the inside walls of the van. Finally, he closed the doors at the back. Sarah felt a moment of panic, being shut in like that. But then she reminded herself: they were going to the zoo, to the zoo, to the zoo. She made a song of this inside herself.

The rest of the family piled into the seats of the van; Amy sat behind her mother and father. Off they went, with a roar of the somewhat cranky motor and a bump-bump, as they backed out of the driveway.

It was a strange trip for Sarah. When she had gone somewhere in the green Chevy, she had sat on the front seat next to her mother or father, fastened tightly with a seat belt, like any other person. She could watch trees and houses and people as they flew past. Sometimes, when they stopped for a red light, she could look right into other cars and see families going somewhere together, two people having an argument, or just a single person going about his or her business.

Now she could only peer out the two rather small back windows of the van and catch a glimpse of the world. It all seemed to be hurrying away from her, and she felt as if she herself were moving swiftly and surely out of the world. And she was all alone. The three people in front talked and laughed together as if she were not even there. It was hot in the van.

"Here we are!" her father announced at last, and Sarah realized that both she and the world around her had stopped moving. And there, two cars away, was Aunt Laura in a bright blue dress, just getting out of her red car.

First, they went along a path between dense, leafy trees, and then there was a wide green lawn, with white flowers scattered along the edge. *How wonderful*, Sarah was saying inside herself.

"Look, there's still some Queen Anne's lace!" Amy exclaimed. She picked one and held it out to Sarah.

Sarah had never seen such lace in a flower—tiny clusters, with a dot of purple in the center. She took her hand off the switch and held the flower while her mother pushed the wheelchair. After a while, her fingers relaxed and the flower dropped down on the path.

As they approached the zoo, Sarah could see a number of families walking in the same direction, on other paths. A group of shouting children on bicycles whizzed by. Older boys and girls danced on the lawn to the tune of a boom box one of them was carrying. Just then, a woman bumped into Sarah's wheelchair as she pulled a little girl along the path.

"Sorry!" she said, and she looked alarmed.

The little girl stared at Sarah with wide, dark eyes. She wore a floppy white hat that looked out of place on her small head. Sarah stared back.

"Sorry!" the woman said again, as she kept pulling the little girl along.

So many people! It was all new to Sarah, exciting. She made burbling sounds in her excitement. But it was frightening, too. She felt so helpless in her wheelchair with all those strong, active people around her.

They were approaching a tall iron fence with sharp points along the top. Beyond the fence, a collection of brick buildings was arranged in a semicircle. Sarah heard a distant roaring—lions perhaps. And then, right before her eyes appeared the most wonderful sight: a man holding a huge bunch of balloons—red, blue, yellow, pink—all bumping and bobbing together up in the air.

"Have a balloon, Sarah!" Aunt Laura said. She bought a red one from the man and tied it to the left arm of Sarah's wheelchair.

Sarah watched the balloon with delight. She could make it jump around by jerking the string. The sounds she made grew louder and louder.

"Quiet, Squib!" Amy said.

Sarah giggled at her and stopped the noise.

"Hasn't Sarah ever had a balloon before?" Aunt Laura asked.

"I guess not," Sarah's father said uncomfortably.

"I want a balloon, too!" Amy put in.

"Don't be a baby," her father told her. "Just go buy one. Didn't you bring your allowance?"

"I forgot."

"Here, go get one," her mother said, and she gave Amy the money.

Amy's balloon was blue. She tried to bump it into Sarah's balloon as they went along.

"Let's see the lions first," Amy suggested.

"Okay," said Aunt Laura. "Lions it is." And they headed for a low brick building inside the fence.

So this was the zoo! Sarah saw tall iron cages along the outside of the building. In the nearest one, a lion with an untidy mane was pacing back and forth. They stopped to watch.

This wasn't at *all* what Sarah had imagined the zoo would be like. She knew there would be fences, and the animals would be behind bars. They mustn't be allowed to wander all over the city. But Sarah had no idea that the cages would be so small. The lion roared and snarled. *No wonder he roars,* Sarah thought. *He can't go anywhere any more than I can.*

In the next cage, a lion without a mane was pacing just like the first one. "That's the lady lion," Aunt Laura said.

They hate those cages, Sarah was thinking. *I would, too.*

People had been crowding around them to see the lions. A boy in blue jeans, walking backwards for fun, crashed his behind into Sarah's wheelchair. Whammo! The wheelchair shook. The boy turned to see what he had hit, and his eyes opened wide.

"What happened to you?" he wanted to know. "Did you have an accident?"

Sarah shook her head, *no.*

"Something else?"

Sarah kept shaking her head. She pointed to her mouth and rang her bell but the boy did not know what she meant.

"You don't want to talk to me? Okay!" he said, and he pushed his way through the crowd and disappeared.

Come back, Sarah wanted to say, *I do want to talk to you! I can only talk with symbols, don't you see?*

No one else had noticed what happened. Amy had met a friend from school and wandered off. Their mother was discussing clothes with Aunt Laura. Sarah's father was standing right beside her but he seemed to be looking off into some faraway distance.

They went on to other animals—zebras, giraffes, elephants, and strange creatures Sarah had never heard of. Some had a small yard in which to run. That was better. The bears had the best place, rocks they could climb over and a cool cave to hide in. Somehow, they never got to the monkeys.

It was hot. They were always in the sun. Sweat began to pour down Sarah's face and drip off her nose. Her mother wiped Sarah's face once and sighed.

Now there were more people watching the bears.

They pressed tight against the fence. Suddenly the little girl with the big white hat was standing beside Sarah, staring again. Her mother hurried over and pulled her away. "Sorry, sorry," she said, looking at Sarah. *All she ever says is "Sorry,"* Sarah said inside herself.

"Let's get something to eat," her father suggested.

Suddenly Sarah knew she *was* hungry. She pushed the switch on her wheelchair, eager to get out of the crowd. The wheelchair didn't move; it couldn't. They were hemmed in by what seemed to Sarah an endless mass of people—tall and short, big and small. She felt squeezed in, squashed, more helpless than the animals in cages. *Get me out of here!* she was saying inside herself. *Get me out!*

"We'll just have to wait," her mother said, but her father did not want to wait.

"Make way, please! Make way!" he called out. Startled, people turned and stared at Sarah. Then, slowly, they began to move away.

"Make way, please!"

Finally, just a few people lingered nearby.

"Let's go, Sarah," her father said, and they started down the wide walkway towards the hot dog stand.

Sarah's head was spinning. Too many people, too many animals. She wanted to go home. Instead, she

71

had to sit in the sun while her father stood in line with her mother and Aunt Laura to buy hot dogs and orange drink. When they finally had the food in paper bags, they found a bench where they could sit in the shade. Amy appeared.

"Got one for me?" she asked, meaning a hot dog.

"Sure," her father said.

Her mother handed Sarah a hot dog in a roll with a paper napkin around it. Sarah took it carefully in her good hand. She didn't like eating with all those people around. Oh well, she had better eat that hot dog. One bite, then another. Her mother held a cup of orange drink with a straw in it, so Sarah could take a sip.

Another bite of hot dog. Then her fingers suddenly lost their grip, and the rest of the hot dog and the roll fell down into the dirt. A tall woman in blue jeans who was passing by picked them up and laid them on Sarah's board.

"There, sweetie," she said, and continued on her way.

Sarah looked at the hot dog. It was grimy. Mustard was mixed with gravel and the roll was torn. She picked it up. Such a mess. How could she eat *that?* While she was asking herself this she felt her fingers loosen and let go. The hot dog rolled off into the same dirt. Again! This was too much. Sarah felt tears in her eyes; she put down her head and howled. People walking by stopped and looked. She didn't see them; she didn't care. She heard her mother saying, "Quiet, Kitten, quiet!" but she couldn't stop.

Sarah's father grabbed the handles of the wheelchair and started pushing it out of the zoo, fast. The others followed. Sarah kept on crying, but not so loudly now.

"I thought you'd *like* the zoo, Squib!" Amy exclaimed.

Sarah looked at Amy and gave another howl.

At the parking lot, Aunt Laura got right into her car.

"Till the next time!" she called out as she drove off.

Sarah's father pulled down the ramp and wheeled her, front first, into the van. He fastened the brake and the straps.

Well, all right, Sarah said to herself. *I don't care if I don't see anything. Just take me home.*

The inside of the van was at least twice as hot as outside. Sarah could hardly breathe. The red balloon, still fastened to the arm of the wheelchair, moved up to the roof of the van, trembled a moment, and exploded with a frightful bang. Sarah screamed.

"End of a perfect trip," said her father.

Nobody said anything else all the way home. When

73

they arrived, Sarah's father yanked open the back doors of the van and pulled out the ramp while Amy unfastened Sarah's wheelchair and undid the brake. Then he dragged the wheelchair down the ramp, without a word or a look, and pushed it onto the sidewalk. Amy ran down the street, calling over her shoulder, "I'm going to see if Sue's home. I'll be back for supper."

In a daze, Sarah's mother had climbed slowly down from the front of the van. Now she grasped the handles of Sarah's wheelchair, as if she had forgotten Sarah could run it herself, and wheeled her around to the back of the house. Bushes whipped across Sarah's face; she was sopping wet with sweat, so uncomfortable already that a few scratches did not matter.

"I've had it," her mother said. "I've simply had it. I can't take anymore. You wait here, Sarah. I'll be back in a little while."

She left Sarah alone in the garden. Sarah had thought she was finished with crying, but she felt tears on her cheeks again. Every inch of her body felt miserable. She needed to go to the bathroom. *This was supposed to be such a lovely day*, she thought, *and I spoiled it for everyone. They'll never take me on a trip again, never*. She closed her eyes, trying to squeeze away the tears. It seemed as if she sat there the longest time. Where was her mother?

Then Sarah heard a soft thud on her symbol board, and she opened her eyes. Wonder of wonders, a little grey kitten was standing there, mewing as it tried to keep its balance. Sarah brought her left hand over to stroke the kitten. She could feel the softness of its fur moving into her hand and up her arm and all through her body—kitten-softness. The kitten mewed once more, then climbed right up onto Sarah's shoulder. There it nuzzled its head into the corner of Sarah's neck and clung to her T-shirt, purring. She stroked it again, gently.

And there was Ruth, standing close to the wheelchair, looking down at her with a smile. She had come so quietly.

"I think what you need is a kitten," she said.

Oh, her father would never let her keep this kitten. Sarah started to cry again.

"You can *have* it, Sarah," Ruth said. "Amy told me what happened about Sue's kitten, and I talked with your mother. She *wants* you to have a kitten. We were just waiting for my Mimi's kittens to get big enough, so we could surprise you."

Her own kitten. Her own, live kitten for a friend, and it wouldn't matter that she couldn't talk. "He's a boy cat. How about a name for him?" Ruth Burroughs said.

Sarah *did* have a name for a boy cat. She had kept on hoping she'd have a kitten *someday*, and she had chosen names—Mitzie for a girl cat, Toby for a boy cat. Now, she spelled out TOBY on her board.

Ruth nodded with approval. "Hello, Toby!" she said.

And then to Sarah, "Look! He's asleep, right on your shoulder. You don't even have to hold him. He feels at home with you already."

She took Sarah's good left hand in hers. Sarah could feel the warmth of the hand that held hers, and something more than warmth. Again, there was no need to put this into words.

6

Never!

"I'm collecting jokes for you, Squib," Amy said, "to help you feel better."

It was afternoon, three days after the disastrous trip to the zoo. Amy had pulled a chair up close to Sarah's wheelchair in the living room. Outside, a deluge of rain poured down; Sarah could hardly see anything out there. She didn't care. It was as if the whole world were just this room, with its big chairs and sofa sitting in shadow, dim and comfortable and safe. Toby was curled up on the sofa, his grey fur gently rising and falling as he slept.

Sarah turned her attention to Amy. A joke.

"Here's another one I got from Sue," Amy went on. It's a riddle, too. How do you keep the house *extra* warm?"

Amy waited only briefly, knowing Sarah probably could not answer that in symbols. "You give it two coats of paint, silly!"

Amy screamed with delight. "It's so funny the way Sue tells it. She says you have to put in the *silly*, that's part of the joke. Two coats of paint, *silly!*"

Sarah rang her bell to add to the fun, and they sat there laughing together, Amy holding her knees with her arms, rocking back and forth, Sarah shaking as much as she could inside the strap that held her upright.

"You should laugh more," Amy said. "It makes you look different."

Sarah made questioning sounds.

"I mean happier," Amy explained.

Well, she was a little happier. She was just beginning to get back to her everyday self after that zoo experience. Her father had not spoken a word to her the whole day after the trip. He had gone to a ball game with friends from his office that afternoon.

One good thing had happened, though—Toby.

"She's going to keep that cat," Sarah's mother had said when her father complained about the extra work. "She needs it."

Amy loved Toby, too. She helped feed him, and she

took care of his litter box. *But he's mine*, Sarah told herself. *My own living, breathing baby kitten.* She could do most of his feeding herself.

After the "zoo day," Sarah's mother had gone about the house in a sort of dream. At meals she gave Sarah her food with hardly a word. If Sarah made a mess, she cleaned up without complaining. Sarah would have liked it better if her mother would fuss a bit. This way she felt as if no one cared.

"Let's get a snack," Amy was saying.

Together, they headed for the dining area. Suddenly, Amy stopped short and flung an arm across Sarah's shoulders, so she stopped, too. Voices in the dining area, so soft they could barely hear. Maybe, Sarah thought, her mother's friend Mrs. Hayes had come over. But no, it was her father; he had come home early without their knowing.

Sarah made more questioning sounds and started up her wheelchair.

"Sh-sh!" Amy whispered, and Sarah stayed right where she was. They both listened. Sarah could hear her mother crying. She moved forward enough so she could see one end of the table in the dining area. Her mother was bent over it, and her shoulders were shaking with sobs. Her father stood nearby.

"I'm just trying to think what's best for all of us," he was saying. "You can't go on like this, so tired all the time."

Sarah's mother stopped crying and sat up. "I can, Tom."

"You're kidding yourself, Liz. It's too much for you, and we can't afford any help. We'll have to send Sarah somewhere. There are good public institutions, you know."

Amy left Sarah sitting in the living room and burst into the dining area. "You *can't* send Sarah away!" she yelled. "She's my sister!"

Her mother and father gaped at Amy with astonishment.

"What are you doing here?" her father demanded.

"Well, I live here," Amy said. "And I don't want you sending my sister away."

"You shouldn't have listened," her father scolded. "We have to talk about this privately."

Her mother got up from the table. "We can't discuss this rationally now," she said. "In fact, I don't see any use of talking about it at all. Sarah isn't going anywhere." She walked down the hall to her bedroom and closed the door. Sarah's father put on a jacket and went out, slamming the front door behind him.

Sarah had sat there listening to all this as if they were talking about someone else. She just felt numb and confused. Gradually, the reality of what her father had said came to her. Why did he want to send her away? Didn't he love her anymore at all?

Her mother didn't want her to go, but perhaps her father could do it anyway—send her someplace, maybe to Plainview, where Ruth Burroughs' Johnnie lived. Where children didn't live with their families. She was too astonished to cry; instead she sat there whimpering a little.

Amy came back. "Well, let's get that snack," she said.

The last thing Sarah wanted just then was to eat, but she would do anything Amy said. Or anyone else. She would be so good and quiet they wouldn't mind having her around. She followed Amy into the kitchen.

She went through the rest of the day carefully doing whatever was expected of her, keeping quiet so no one would think she was too much trouble.

"Cheer *up*, Squib!" Amy said at supper.

Sarah had nothing to say. She had felt all day a great yearning for her mother's love; her whole body tingled with it. This was a lonely feeling, and she kept it to herself.

When her mother put her to bed that night, she

seemed to be her loving self again. As soon as Sarah was settled, she sat on the edge of the bed and held her close for a long time.

"I love you so much, Kitten," she said. "I need you as much as you need me."

Her mother needed *her*? This did not make sense to Sarah, but she felt the love that went with the words. She looked into her mother's eyes, "ordinary brown eyes," her mother had called them, and with her good hand she gently stroked her mother's hair—brown, too.

"You've been unhappy, Kitten," her mother went on. "I know. But you couldn't help what happened at the zoo. We shouldn't have taken you there on such a hot and busy day. We won't make that mistake again."

Her mother let Sarah fall gently back onto the pillow and smoothed the sheet under her chin. She was going to say good night, but Sarah did not want to say good night. She had something more important than the zoo on her mind.

"Agghh," she said gently, and pointed to her mouth.

Her mother knew what that meant. She propped Sarah up, brought the symbol board, and held it so Sarah could point.

"*Mama,*" Sarah said, "*I'm afraid. Will my father make*

me go away?"

Again a hug, and the warm love that went with it.

"Never, Kitten, never as long as I'm here. I thought you knew that."

"I love you, Mama."

Now perhaps it was time for sleep. Sarah lay still. "Good night"—and Sarah's mother tiptoed out of the room, as if she thought Sarah was already asleep.

But Sarah was not ready for sleep. She looked over at the windows, dim in the approaching darkness. The shades had been pulled down, but the curtain stirred where one window was open. The rain had stopped. Voices from the yard next door floated in. The whole big world was out there—people, lights in the darkness, voices, and song.

As she lay there waiting for sleep, Sarah thought, *I'm just like anyone else now. People everywhere, every night, lie quietly in bed and go to sleep.*

7

Terrible Edgar
Does His Thing

School was getting closer and closer; it was only a week away now. Sarah wanted to practice the trip down the street toward her new school. Her mother said, "All right, but I'd better go with you."

"*No!*" Sarah insisted. "*Mothers don't go to school with big children.*"

She knew, though, that her mother *was* going to be at school with her, right in the classroom. She had gotten a job as a teacher's aide, so she would be there to take Sarah to the bathroom and help her in gym. She would go home with her at noon, too, and give her lunch.

"*Do you have to come?*" Sarah had asked.

"Someone has to help you," her mother said. "It's not like Ingleside. I'll help the teacher, too."

"*I'm not a baby.*"

"I know. You want to do everything yourself. But you can't, Kitten. That's a fact of life you'll have to live with. I'll try to keep hands off except when you really need me."

"*Promise?*"

"Promise."

Now her mother said, "There's something else you haven't thought of. What about Edgar? Suppose he bothers you?"

Edgar—the terrible Edgar, Amy called him. He'd been away at camp all summer, and Sarah had almost forgotten him. Now he would be home. She recalled the time when Amy had come home from school crying—Amy, her tough, self-confident sister, who hardly ever cried.

"It's that bully, Edgar Hoffman, down the street," she had sobbed. "He follows me home from school and yells, 'Ya-ya-ya, how's your funny sister?'"

"Don't pay any attention," her mother said.

"I try," Amy said. "But he's so awful. Today I hit him, and he hit me back."

"I'll speak to his mother."

"No!" Amy protested. "It would only make things worse."

Edgar lived two houses down the street from the

Bennetts, and Sarah had seen him now and then when she was out on the street. She knew that he was in Amy's class at school. Until she heard about Amy's trouble with him, Sarah had thought Edgar looked rather nice; she liked his shaggy brown hair and the way he walked, sort of hopping along. Maybe, she had thought, he would be her friend. No chance of that now.

Still, she didn't think he'd be mean enough to do anything to *her*. People might hurt her feelings, but mostly they meant to help. So, when her mother said, "What about Edgar?" she answered, "*I want to try.*"

"Well. . ." her mother said.

Sarah knew it was hard for her mother to let her go. Ever since she had been a baby, her mother had given so much of her time, so much of her love, to taking care of Sarah.

She pointed to just two symbols, saying, "*I know.*"

The next afternoon she told her mother, "*Now, I'll try,*" and she was sure her mother knew what she meant. She pushed open the screen door, and off she went, down the ramp, onto the sidewalk.

Sarah knew every house on their side of the street. Their own seemed to her the prettiest, with its neat grey shingles and red door. Next, going towards her school, was an important-looking red brick house with a big lawn. Until just a month ago the house had been neatly kept, the lawn always mowed, the hedge trimmed. Now the lawn was like a meadow, all high grass and wildflowers. The old couple who had lived there had gone to live with their daughter.

Then the Hoffmans'. The house itself was less tidy than the brick one; it was an old house with grey paint peeling off the sides. The front porch sagged. The lawn had yellow dandelions scattered through it. Sarah liked the dandelions. "They are flowers," Ruth Burroughs had told her, "not just weeds." Still, Sarah wondered if all those dandelions belonged in a lawn.

Before she even reached the house she saw Edgar out in front, pulling up weeds around the bushes. Quietly, Sarah kept on. Edgar did not see her; he was bent double, eyes on the ground. He straightened up just as Sarah wheeled herself past the row of bushes where he was working. For a moment their eyes met.

Then: "Ya-ya-ya, Amy's funny sister!" he taunted.

Sarah's mother had told Amy to pay no attention when he talked like that. All right, that was what she'd do. But then Edgar was rushing up to her, snarling. He grabbed the left arm of her wheelchair, and she couldn't move.

"Get off this street!" he yelled. "You hadn't ought to be here!"

Sarah took her hand off the switch and banged it down hard on Edgar's hand. "Ow!" he yelled, but he didn't let go. Sarah was scared. Suddenly her mother was there. She must have been watching all the time.

"Stop it, Edgar!" she said. "Stop it or there's going to be trouble." Edgar did not say another word. He let go of the arm of the wheelchair and went back to his weeding.

"Sarah, listen to me," her mother said. "You go on home. I'm going in to talk with Edgar's mother."

She walked right past Edgar, where he bent among the shrubbery, and onto the Hoffman porch, where she rang the doorbell. Sarah watched her go inside as someone opened the door. Then she turned her wheelchair around and headed for home.

Her mother came home about a half-hour later and found her in her room, just staring out the window.

"You really *can't* go down the street alone, Kitten," she said. "I'm sorry. I just don't see what we can do about Edgar."

Why, Mama? Sarah wanted to ask. *Why?* Surely her mother, who had protected her all these years, could stop Edgar from tormenting her when she wanted to go down the street by herself.

"I'm sorry," her mother said again.

Sarah turned her wheelchair away. This was the first time she could ever remember her mother not being able to get other people to understand. It was scary, knowing this could happen.

And what about Edgar's mother? Why couldn't *she* help?

Her mother had something to say about that at dinnertime. "I had a talk with Edgar Hoffman's mother," she told the family. "He was bothering Sarah."

"Oh?" her father said.

"That poor woman has a real problem," her mother went on. "She had a drink in one hand when she answered the door, and she wobbled. I think she hardly even heard what I said."

"You mean she was drunk?" Sarah thought her father found this rather funny.

"Well, I guess she was. No wonder she can't manage Edgar."

"I *told* you not to go," Amy put in.

Her mother ignored that. "What can we do to help, Tom?"

"There's nothing we can do, Liz. It's *their* problem."

"I suppose it is," Sarah's mother said, frowning, and

she turned away.

The next Saturday morning, Sarah's mother said she was going shopping with Aunt Laura. "Amy will stay with you," her mother said. "We'll be back for lunch."

Where would her father be, Sarah wondered. As if in answer, her father said, "Harry Burroughs wants me to help him fix his back steps. I'll be right next door if anyone needs me."

"You can take Sarah up to the woods if you want," her mother said to Amy.

Sarah shook her head. She used to love the woods, but now it bothered her too much that she couldn't go down those mysterious, shaded paths.

Amy shrugged. "Where else is there to go?"

Nobody answered that one. Aunt Laura honked the horn outside, and Sarah's mother waved good-bye as they went off in the red car.

"Do you want to go out in the garden?" Amy asked Sarah.

Not today. She wanted something special to happen.

"You're making it kind of hard, Squib," Amy protested.

Sarah was silent, waiting. A bee bumbled against the screen in the window. *No, no, not here,* Sarah wanted to tell him. *Go find a flower.*

"I know what," Amy said. "We'll go down to the store on the corner. I'll buy you an ice cream pop."

Wonderful. It was a long time since Sarah had been to the store. But what about Edgar? How could Amy manage him if his own mother couldn't, or her mother?

Amy knew what was on her mind. "Don't worry about Edgar," she said. "There's a big Boy Scout bash today, and he's sure to be there."

Sarah hoped he was.

"Okay?" Amy was asking. Sarah nodded. Of course, okay.

"Let's go then, Squib," Amy said, and together they headed down the ramp, down the street, Sarah going much faster than she dared when her mother was around. She took a quick look at the big brick house as they went by, enough to see that a plainly lettered sign had been attached to a column near the front door: FOR SALE.

"I wonder who'll move in," Amy commented.

As they passed the Hoffman house, Sarah thought she heard someone crying inside. She didn't know if Amy heard, she seemed in such a hurry.

The local grocery was small and definitely not a place for wheelchairs. There were two steps at the entrance, and inside, the aisles were narrow and crowded with shelves of food. Amy left Sarah sitting outside. After a while, two women who lived on her street came out with bags of groceries and started talking about her.

"Poor thing, she can't talk," one said.

"Isn't that awful," the other went on. "Her mother must be worn out taking care of her."

Amy appeared just then with their ice cream pops; she had heard what they said. "She can *hear* every word you say," she told the women.

Sarah felt like cheering. *That's telling them!*

The women mumbled something about being sorry and scuttled up the street.

Sarah and Amy ate their pops right there, in front of the store. By the time they were finished, Sarah's pink shirt was spattered with bits of chocolate, and ice cream had dribbled down her chin. Amy went inside to get more napkins.

"I can always tell when you've had fun, Squib," she said, as she helped Sarah wipe her face.

Then, "We'd better get home before Mama and Aunt Laura do."

They didn't really hurry back, though. The ice cream pops felt good inside them, the morning sun had grown warmer, and it was comfortable just to wander slowly along. When they came to the Hoffman house, Sarah tried to look inside, still wondering who had been crying.

Then it happened. Edgar appeared, as if out of nowhere.

"You get out of here!" he yelled as he ran towards them.

"Shut up, Edgar!" Amy yelled back. "We have as much right to be here as you have."

"Not with that funny sister of yours!" He grabbed an arm of Sarah's wheelchair and started shaking it. It was the right arm this time; Sarah couldn't even try to push him off.

Amy was quick. First she fastened the brake of the wheelchair, then she started pounding Edgar on the back. But he kept on shaking the wheelchair, harder now. Crash! It went over, too fast for Sarah to know what was happening. Her head hit the sidewalk, hard. The strap that held her against the back of the wheelchair cut into her stomach. Her right arm was pinned under the wheel.

At first Sarah couldn't make a sound. Then she started screaming. Amy was tugging at the wheelchair, trying to pull it upright. It was too heavy. Edgar stood there, staring, as if he could not take in what had happened.

Just then, Aunt Laura and Sarah's mother drove up. They screeched to a stop, and Sarah's mother rushed over to her.

"It's all right, Kitten," she said. "We'll get you up."

Aunt Laura helped, and with Amy holding Sarah's head, they heaved the wheelchair upright. Sarah's mother straightened the strap around Sarah's middle and patted her face.

"It's all right, Kitten," she said again.

Then she turned on Edgar. "What's the *matter* with you, Edgar Hoffman, picking on a little girl in a wheelchair?"

Edgar stopped staring. "Well, she hadn't ought to be on the street."

A thin little woman came out of the house and walked uncertainly down the front walk. "Don't you bother Edgar," she said in a sing-song voice.

"Mrs. Hoffman," Sarah's mother said, "he knocked over Sarah's wheelchair."

"Oh," Edgar's mother replied. "Well, you see, it bothers him, seeing someone like that."

"Mrs. Hoffman," Sarah's mother went on, and Sarah could tell she was angry. "She's a person with feelings like anyone else. And she has a right to go up and down this street without being attacked."

Mrs. Hoffman laughed softly and brushed back a wisp of blond hair from her face.

"Oh," she said again. And then suddenly she turned, tripped on the edge of the walk, and sat down on the lawn among the dandelions.

"Let's go home," Sarah's mother said.

Sarah had been too stunned at first to feel anything. Now her forehead began to hurt. Her right hand tingled. She let her mother push the wheelchair towards home, with Amy walking alongside.

Aunt Laura got into her car. "I'll see you at the house," she called out.

"Mama, I'm sorry," Amy was saying. "Mama, I thought Edgar wasn't home."

"Well, he was," her mother said. "Next time don't go *this* way with Sarah."

Sarah was crying. She could hear Amy crying, too. The street, with its familiar houses, was just a blur as they hurried along.

Then Amy stopped crying. "Look!" she said. "She has a big bump on her head!"

Sarah touched her forehead where it hurt. She felt a swelling nearly as big as an egg. She whimpered.

"Don't worry, Kitten," her mother said. "It won't stay that way."

When they got home, Aunt Laura was telling Sarah's father what had happened.

"This is too much!" he exclaimed. "It's time something was done."

"Just *what?*" Aunt Laura asked. And then, without waiting for an answer, she said she'd be going along, and off she went.

Amy went into her room and closed the door.

Sarah's mother took her straight to her room. "You'd better lie down while I get lunch, Kitten," she said. "I'll bring some ice for that bump on your head."

She helped Sarah onto her bed. Sarah lay on her back, trying to relax her muscles the way the physical therapist in school had taught her. It was hard. Every inch of her body felt tense and stiff. Her head throbbed.

There was a soft thud as Toby landed on the bed beside her. Sarah stroked his head and tickled his throat to make him purr. He curled up against the curve of her arm, sure enough purring.

She felt safe here, on her own bed, in her familiar room. Countless times as she lay on this bed she had looked across the room to the shadowy shape of the doorway, waiting for her mother to come with words of love and comfort.

Now her mother came carrying an ice pack by its screw top. "This is *really* cold," she said. "We'll get that bump shrunk, all right."

She put the ice pack on Sarah's forehead. It made Sarah shiver, but almost at once her head stopped hurting. Then her mother gently stroked Sarah's arms and legs.

"There, Kitten," she said. "That will make you feel better."

She kissed Sarah on the cheek and left her alone.

Sarah found that now she could relax without even trying. *That's my mother*, she thought. *She always knows what to do. Never mind about Edgar, never mind.*

A lullaby her mother used to sing to her was going around and around in her head: "Hush, little baby, don't say a word . . ."

Sarah wondered how her mother had felt when she discovered that her own little baby she loved so much would never say a word and never walk. It was a good thing her mother had Amy. *She* was all right.

"Special treat, you're having lunch in bed," her mother said as she appeared with a tray.

Lunch in bed! She really was special today. With her good hand, she blew her mother a kiss.

8

New School; New People

Sarah's teacher at Ingleside had made a new symbol board for her to use at her new school. It was bigger than the one she'd been using, and it had many more symbols. Sarah chose the symbols herself, from a set of printed "symbol stamps." These were sticky on the back. Her teacher stuck each one onto an empty square on the board, until most of the squares were covered. One row of squares was left empty for future use.

Sarah now had three hundred symbols. They were arranged in groups, to make them easier to use. People and things were together, and these were colored yellow. Symbols that meant any kind of action, or just being, were colored green. Those that told what something was like, or how you felt, were placed together and always colored blue.

The symbols on her new board were a little smaller than the ones Sarah was used to; they had to be, to get so many on the board. Many were new to Sarah. She didn't expect to have any trouble learning them. *After all*, she said to herself, *I can see.*

The letters of the alphabet appeared in a neat row just above the symbols, as before. In the upper left corner, in a circle, was a big symbol for "NO": **−!!** In the upper right corner, "YES": **+!!** Sarah liked that.

Sarah had been talking whole sentences in symbols for several years. She could draw them on paper, too. Of course, now she could read, and she could write words, like anyone her age. But the quickest way of getting her ideas across was still by pointing at symbols.

She could say whether something was happening in the past, right now, or in the future. She liked knowing how separate symbols had been put together to make compound symbols.

A friend was a "person" plus "like":

A teacher was a "person who gives knowledge":

$$\perp \, \text{Ϙ} \, \square$$

A wheelchair, of course, was a "chair" with a "wheel":

A cloud was "water" $\sim$ plus the "sky" — like this: $\sim$

Sometimes Sarah combined symbols herself, to get a new meaning. Then, whoever was watching had to think a bit to get what she meant. Her mother was pretty good at this.

Sarah used some sentences over and over again.

"I am happy": $\perp_1 \ \hat{\Phi} \ \heartsuit\!\!\!\!\vee \, \uparrow$ Or sometimes, "I am upset": $\perp_1 \ \hat{\Phi} \ \heartsuit\!\!\!\!\vee \uparrow\downarrow$

Now and then, "sad": $\heartsuit\!\!\!\!\vee \downarrow$

She liked to say, "I love my mother and father":

$$\perp_1 \ \overset{\wedge}{\ominus}\!\!\rightarrow \ \perp_{1+} \ \hat{\triangle} \ + \ \wedge$$

"My sister, too,": $\perp_{1+} \quad \hat{\triangle}_2 \quad +$

101

She could explain how these symbols were made.

⊥₁ is "person number 1" (of course). The lines like this ∧ at the top of the symbols for mother and father look like a roof. A roof protects a house; the mother and father protect the family.

When anyone asked about the heart symbol and the arrows, Sarah would say in symbols:

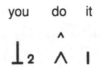

Figure it out yourself.

Sarah's mother had pasted the pictures of her family, with their names, in a row near the top of her board. There were extra spaces for new friends. A narrow strip across the top read, "My name is Sarah Bennett. I communicate with Blissymbols."

✳ ✳ ✳

Finally, the first day of school came, sunny and warm. Sarah had chosen to wear her best blue jeans and a plain white blouse with a red and blue scarf—nice, but not too flashy. She steered her wheelchair down the street quite early, when there would surely be only a few children on the street. Her mother walked beside her, silent most of the way. Sarah tried to look as if she were really going by herself, not helped by her mother. There was a funny feeling in her stomach; she was scared.

She saw two children on their way, a brother and sister who lived up near the woods. Sarah knew them; she waved, but they seemed too busy to notice. They hurried on.

At last, Sarah and her mother turned the corner at the end of the street. There, past the corner store, was Jacobson Middle School, a plain yellow brick building, all on one floor. There were tidy, clipped bushes all around.

"Nearly there," her mother said. "You're going to like this school, Kitten."

Sarah had been waiting impatiently all summer for this day, but now she wasn't so sure it was what she wanted.

It was too late to turn back; the big front door of the school was just ahead of them. A group of girls and boys hurried past; one of them opened the door, and they disappeared inside.

That's a heavy door, Sarah was thinking. *Who will open it for me?* She and her mother made their way up the ramp that led to the door, and of course, this time, her mother opened the door. As so often happened, her mother knew what Sarah was thinking.

"There'll always be someone to open the door when I'm not with you," she said. "So many children and teachers come in the morning."

Sarah nodded. There would be times like that.

They were in the hallway. This was nothing like Ingleside. There was a buzz of talk all over as groups of children came together. One boy chased another until a teacher yelled at them to stop. A girl in a red-and-white striped dress came through the big door. "Hi, Sarah!" she said. "Coming to this school now?" Sarah nodded; another girl from her street.

A dark-haired boy stood and stared at Sarah. *Haven't you ever seen anyone in a wheelchair?* she wanted to say. She blinked and turned away.

None of this would ever have happened at Ingleside. There, the vans carrying children in wheelchairs drove up to a special wide door at the side of the school building. One by one, the children proceeded quietly down the hallway to their classrooms, some having their wheelchairs pushed by a teacher or a helper who had been waiting for them. Children who could walk came in another door, but there were never as many as at Jacobson.

Now, Sarah was following her mother down the hall to her classroom. Her mother knew the way; she had been there before to help the teacher get the room ready for the first day of school.

Into the classroom. Sarah's first impression was of bright light and cheerful colors. Yellow ruffled curtains covered the bottom part of the tall windows. Sarah glanced up through a window. All she could see was sky and the tops of trees, but a great feeling of longing suddenly came over her. She belonged out there. What was she doing in here?

"Mrs. Stevens wants to say hello," Sarah's mother was saying. "Your teacher."

Of course, her teacher. Sarah's mother had told Sarah about her. Sarah pulled her attention away from the window.

"Hello, Sarah. I'm glad you're here." Mrs. Stevens had straight blond hair falling to her shoulders; she was smiling. That was all Sarah noticed at first.

"I've been learning Blissymbols, Sarah," Mrs. Stevens said, "so you can talk to me."

"Hello. Thank you. Hello, S.," Sarah said in symbols. She wasn't quite sure what she was pointing to, but that didn't seem to bother Mrs. Stevens.

"I've put symbols up on the wall, too," Mrs. Stevens

went on. The other children may want to learn them."

There they were, some of the symbols Sarah knew so well:

paper	pencil	book	desk	chair	picture

girl	boy	talk	read	sing	house

This school might be all right, after all. Sarah looked around the room. There were seven desks and chairs in a circle, and a space in the circle—for her wheelchair? Would she be the only child in a wheelchair?

Other children were arriving. Sarah counted; five so far. They seemed to know each other already. Mrs. Stevens introduced them to Sarah, but Sarah couldn't tell one from another at first. Two boys didn't say anything at all. They stared at Sarah. One was dark-skinned, with dark, deep eyes; the other was pale and blue-eyed. There was a small, silent girl, too; she turned away. Sarah wondered: *Can't they speak? Or don't they want to?*

Another girl seemed to talk all the time. She was thin, with straggly hair that looked as if no one combed it. She spoke so fast that Sarah could not figure out what she said. But Sarah liked her name: Jennifer.

A boy they called Joe stood near the door by himself, saying over and over again, "I won't, I won't."

Won't what? Sarah wondered. This boy had shaggy brown hair, like Edgar's, but he was not like Edgar any other way. Edgar was short and heavy—tubby, Amy had said. Joe was tall and thin.

School began. First, Mrs. Stevens asked every child to say something about vacation. This was like Ingleside, except that there, of course, "talking" was in symbols. Here, several children would not say anything at all. When it was her turn, Sarah said in symbols, *"My summer was busy. We went on a trip."* Mrs. Stevens read Sarah's message from her board as Sarah pointed. A short message; that was all she felt like saying right now.

Then Mrs. Stevens showed the children the symbols on the wall and told them what they meant. "Some of you can read the word above each symbol," she said. "Sarah can read the symbols, too, and you can learn them. Then Sarah can talk with all of you."

"Thanks, thanks," Sarah said by pointing. Mrs. Stevens came over and looked, and she smiled her lovely smile.

The morning went on, mostly with Mrs. Stevens talking about the work they would all be doing. Sarah was feeling a bit confused; so much would be new.

Then recess time. Sarah had looked forward to this.

"Recess is totally fun," Amy had told her. "All the classes in your grade go out together and play games."

At Ingleside, the children had played games and danced in wheelchairs. The Virginia Reel was Sarah's favorite dance. Now she wanted to see what "regular" children would do.

"Mr. Green is in charge of playground," Mrs. Stevens said. "If you need anything, ask him."

Sarah started out the door and down the hall. Her mother was beside her. "*No!*" Sarah said, pointing to her board.

"Don't you want me to go with you?" her mother whispered to her.

"*No.*"

Her mother frowned. "Just the first time?"

"*No.*"

"Be careful, then." Her mother reluctantly turned away.

The playground, in back of the school building, was much bigger than Sarah had expected. Most of it was covered with cement; that was good for wheelchairs.

There were some lines painted on the cement, for some game, Sarah supposed. And at the far end of the play-ground, in front of a tall fence, she saw two baskets for basketball. Sarah had seen *that* game on television.

There were a few big trees—one of them a maple like the trees along her street. They were on the other side of the fence that surrounded the playground, but here and there they gave some welcome shade.

It was hot. Sarah moved gratefully into the shade. She had been there about a minute when she was sur-rounded by excited children, pushing tight against her wheelchair.

"Hey, look what she's got!" someone yelled.

Her symbol board was practically hidden from sight as curious fingers poked and pointed.

"Show us how it works!" a girl insisted. She saw the bell attached to the arm of Sarah's wheelchair and rang it merrily.

How could she show them anything? She could hardly see the board herself, and her good arm was pinned against it. This was too much like the time when she was stuck in a crowd at the zoo.

She felt hot all over. There wasn't a single familiar face among those crowded around her.

Somehow she got her good arm loose and pushed

her switch. The wheelchair did not move. She pushed harder. They wouldn't let her move, that was the trouble. All those kids. Where was Mr. Green?

They were all talking at once. She could no longer figure out what they were saying. Finally, a girl's voice could be heard above the others. "C'mon, kids, let her alone. She can't even move her wheelchair."

The children scattered almost as quickly as they had gathered. Sarah sat limply in her wheelchair, staring ahead. That must be Mr. Green who was getting the kids together on the other side of the playground. He was a tall, dark-skinned man carrying two basketballs. Children lined up to "throw a basket," boys and girls in separate lines. Sarah recognized one or two of the children in her class. Joe seemed full of enthusiasm now, bouncing up and down.

The girl who had spoken was still standing by Sarah's wheelchair. She was round-faced, with a snub nose and teeth that stuck out when she smiled.

"My name's Maggie," she said. "What's yours?"

Sarah pointed to the words printed on her board: *"My name is Sarah Bennett."* Then she pointed to *"Thank you,"* and Maggie got the idea right away.

"I'll be your friend," Maggie said. "You'll need one in a new school."

Sarah wanted to talk with her some more, but Mr. Green was hurrying over, leaving the two lines of children to throw baskets by themselves.

"Welcome, Sarah!" he said. "I know you can't throw baskets, but we'll have some games you can play, too. I'll talk to you about it later."

Then he turned to Maggie. "C'mon, Maggie! Play ball!"

"I hate throwing baskets," Maggie confided to Sarah, but she walked slowly across the playground and lined up with the other girls. Sarah watched. She was fascinated by the way Maggie walked. No one else she knew walked like that, with toes pointing in.

✳ ✳ ✳

It wasn't long before Sarah was happier in Jacobson School than she had ever expected to be. She felt so grown up, going all the way to school in her wheelchair and coming home for lunch. She had told her mother she wanted to go to school by herself, and after the first few days she would go all the way alone. Her mother would follow, but not close, so they wouldn't seem to know each other.

Most mornings, as Sarah set out, Ruth Burroughs would open her front door and wave.

"Happy day, Sarah!" she would call out, and Sarah

111

would wave back cheerfully.

Sarah's mother tried hard to let her alone in school; Sarah could see that. She kept busy helping the teacher and the other children. Sometimes, though, she would forget and try to help Sarah, too. She would point out a symbol she knew Sarah was looking for, or she would offer to spell a word.

"You're not my teacher," Sarah would tell her.

Finally, they agreed on a signal. When Sarah wanted her mother to let her alone, she would push her whole arm across the symbol board. Her mother would go away. Once or twice when this happened, Sarah thought she saw tears in her mother's eyes.

Sarah liked to watch Mrs. Stevens with the other children. She was so patient; slowly, one step at a time, she would help them forget they were scared. Sarah especially liked to watch Jim, one of the boys she had thought couldn't speak. He was the smallest boy in the class, and he came to school in patched-up jeans and bright-colored T-shirts. At first he just sat quietly in his seat, with a faraway look. Then Mrs. Stevens put a book on his desk. It looked to Sarah like a storybook, pretty easy to read, with a picture of bears on the cover.

"For you, Jim," Mrs. Stevens said.

"I can't read," he told her, and that was the first thing

he had said in that room.

"I know," Mrs. Stevens said. "I can help you learn."

Jennifer, who talked a lot, could read as well as Sarah. They played games together and did exercises in workbooks. But Jennifer couldn't seem to sit still. She interrupted herself by getting up to walk around the room, or by pulling her long hair over her face and then throwing it back.

Joe kept muttering all of the first week. "This stuff is for the birds," he complained. Then, one day when Sarah was talking to Mrs. Stevens with her symbols, Joe came over and looked, first at Sarah's symbols, then at the ones on the wall.

"I guess I could learn *those*," he said.

Symbols first, then words. Sarah helped Joe learn; he would say a word, and she would show him the symbol. *She* was being a teacher. This was something new and wonderful.

"Hey," Joe said one day, "if I can learn symbols, why can't I learn to read?"

"You can," Mrs. Stevens said.

And so the class progressed, all of them learning about symbols, what they meant, how they were put together; most of them reading, though some better than others.

There were other subjects, of course—math, social studies, music, English, and creative writing, which meant writing your own stories and poems. Sarah loved that. When she had been in sixth grade for two weeks, Mrs. Stevens said to the children, "Suppose you could have—or be—anything you wanted. What would that be? Write about it."

"I want to talk with my voice," Sarah wrote. "I want to walk down the street and no one notices because I am like anyone else. I want to sit myself on the toilet and get myself into bed so my mother won't have to work so hard."

They painted pictures, too, not with their fingers as they had at Ingleside, but with brushes dipped in bright-colored poster paints. It was hard for Sarah to hold a brush. Her mother wanted to help her, but Sarah shook her head. Finally Mrs. Stevens tied the brush to Sarah's hand with a red ribbon.

"Now you can paint with your whole arm," she said.

One time Sarah painted a bird with feathers in many colors, all curling around.

"That's a *bird?*" Jennifer said.

Never mind, Sarah told herself. The real bird she wanted to paint was in her head, a bright, glorious creature ready to take off into the sky, as she sometimes did in her dreams.

For several days Sarah continued to feel strange on the playground at recess time. She was the only child in a wheelchair in all that crowd. Then she discovered that could make her special. She would go whizzing across the cement part of the playground with admiring boys and girls following after.

Mr. Green did try to include her in circle games, and there was always someone to fool around with when they had free time—Maggie especially. She brought a pad of paper and pencils and showed Sarah how to play tic-tac-toe by first drawing, then pointing; they did it nearly every day. And Sarah taught Maggie symbols, a few at a time.

At home, Sarah told Amy and their father about school.

"Seven children, besides me," she said after her first day. *"Four can read."*

"Only four, Squib!" Amy exclaimed.

"These are special children," Sarah's mother said.

Aunt Laura had come to dinner. "Special misfits, it sounds like to me," she said.

"Laura, what do you mean by *that?*" Sarah's mother protested.

"No one around here ever knows what I mean,"

Aunt Laura complained.

Sarah knew what misfits were. Aunt Laura would have called Paul, at Ingleside, a misfit, too. But that wasn't what he was to Sarah. He was her loving friend. Sarah still thought of Paul sometimes; she remembered Ingleside.

"Can we visit my other school?" she asked her mother.

"Sometime," was the answer.

But they never did.

9

Hello, Boy-J.
Hello, Girl-S.

"You won't need me anymore when you go on trips, will you?" Sarah's father said, and her mother replied, "You mean you'd rather go to the ball game."

"Well. . ." her father said.

So they *were* going on trips after all. Sarah banged on her wheelchair tray to show her approval.

They went first to the park where Amy had gone in the summer on her Girl Scout trip. "Sarah wanted to go, too, that time," her mother said. Now there were just the three of them—Sarah, Amy, and their mother.

The idea of going anywhere would have been a pleasure to Sarah, but she was disappointed in the park. She had imagined broad meadows and wide paths through the woods, where even she could go. But there was nothing for a child in a wheelchair, just ballfields with trampled grass, swings, a tall jungle gym, and a few picnic tables under occasional trees. Still, it was a trip; it got her away from home.

They took shorter trips to show Sarah the city, and her class went to the natural history museum in a van with an elevator just for her. This was something like the trips her class at Ingleside used to take. Sarah stared with amazement at the skeletons of dinosaurs and strange prehistoric birds while Jennifer pranced about, saying, "Look at *this!*"

Ruth Burroughs kept telling Sarah about Johnnie, and at last, in October, Sarah's mother said they would go to Plainview the next Saturday.

Sarah wasn't sure she wanted to see this place where Johnnie lived.

"Does he like *living there?"* she asked Ruth Burroughs.

"Of course," Ruth answered. "Wait until you see."

Sarah persisted. *"Without family?"*

"It's like living with a great big family."

"I see," Sarah said, but she did not see.

That Saturday was a brisk day, with bright maple leaves blowing around the house and across the street. They left for Plainview in the van in the early afternoon—Sarah, her mother, and Ruth Burroughs. Amy had gone to Sue's.

Ruth kept telling Sarah about Plainview.

"Too bad it isn't spring," she said. "You'd love all those daffodils in the gardens."

Sarah hardly listened. She was wondering about Johnnie. Would he be helpless, like some of the children at Ingleside, needing someone to push his wheelchair? Or could he get around by himself, the way she did? Could he talk clearly enough so she could understand him?

She was wearing a new navy blue blazer and a red blouse Ruth had made for her. The blouse had velcro on both sides of the front opening, so she could fasten and unfasten it herself; Ruth had thought of that. Her full skirt covered her knees, and her legs below that sported red knee socks, and shoes. No one could tell, just by looking at these legs, that she couldn't move them at all.

Plainview was on the outskirts of the city; it took them nearly an hour to get there. At last, "Here we are!" Ruth exclaimed.

The building they approached was so big, six stories high—Sarah counted as she looked out the back of the van—red brick, with windows everywhere. *A lot of people must be living in there,* Sarah thought. *Do they all have to live in an institution? Is that what they wanted?*

They drove between rows of bushes. "Azalea," Ruth said. "Lovely when it blooms in the spring."

They stopped in front of the building, and Sarah's mother pulled the ramp down from inside the van. Sarah steered her way safely down onto a cement walkway—she could do that herself now. She found herself with Ruth, facing a big double glass door, but she did not want to see, yet, what was behind it. Her mother was parking the van—"behind the azaleas," Ruth said. When Sarah's mother joined them, they all went towards that door. It sprang open before them. This was no surprise to Sarah; the same thing had happened at Ingleside. Through the door, then, and into a spacious area Ruth said was the lobby. A dark-skinned woman in a white dress sat behind a curved desk with two telephones on it.

"I'll tell Johnnie you're here," she said, after Ruth spoke to her.

The lobby opened onto a long hallway. A boy and girl went by together, holding hands, each in a motorized wheelchair. A nurse pushed a sort of bed with wheels on which a little girl lay, covered up to her neck with a sheet. Her face was almost as white as the sheet.

Then the elevator door across the hall opened, and a boy in a wheelchair came out and steered right towards them. Johnnie! He didn't look at all the way Sarah had imagined. She knew he was two years older than herself, but somehow she had thought he would look like the boys at Ingleside, small and bent over, perhaps wobbling a little. Johnnie sat up straight in his wheelchair without even a strap to hold him, and he gave them a wide, straight grin under a mass of dark, curly hair. And his eyes! Darker than any she had ever seen.

"Hi, Aunt Ruth!" he said, and she gave him a kiss. Then he shook hands with Sarah and her mother.

He can do nearly anything, Sarah was thinking—*except walk.* But then she saw that his left hand lay still and useless in his lap, like her right one.

For a few minutes Johnnie and the two women talked about the weather, and how he was getting along, and "How's your mother, Johnnie?" Sarah began to wonder why she was there.

Then Johnnie turned to her. "Let's see your symbols, Sarah," he said. He certainly spoke clearly.

She pointed at her symbol board. Johnnie moved his wheelchair next to hers and looked. "Oh, good," he said. "You have words, too. I can read them."

Sarah pointed.

Hello   boy-J

O→←   ⊰J

Johnnie let out a whoop. "Hello, girl-S."

Sarah laughed. But then she did not know what else to say.

"Why don't you take Sarah to the gardens?" Ruth asked. "She could see how they're set up, even if yours hasn't any flowers yet."

"Sure," he said. "Come with me, Sarah."

Before she had time to think about it, she and Johnnie were going down a long hallway side by side and out another door that opened for them. They were in a garden, but this was an ordinary one, on ground level. Masses of flowers, bright yellow and white, bloomed along the walkway.

"Chrysanthemums," Johnnie said. "The last flowers of all."

Sarah nodded. She knew about chrysanthemums; Ruth had some that looked like pink daisies, near her back door.

"I'll show you *my* garden," Johnnie was saying, "but you'll have to come in the spring to see flowers in it."

The paths were wide enough for two wheelchairs and covered with smooth concrete. Going along them was easy.

"This way!" Johnnie said. She followed him down a side path, and there were the gardens Ruth had told her about: narrow beds of earth on a brick wall just high enough so a person in a wheelchair could easily reach them. Sarah had not dreamed there could really be gardens for people like her. Did you have to live in an institution to have a garden like that?

She saw more chrysanthemums in the first raised flower bed they passed. The plants had little round, pale yellow blossoms.

"Buttons," Johnnie commented.

I like those best, Sarah said inside herself, wishing she could say this to Johnnie. But he was hurrying her along.

There was a square, bricked-over space at the end of each flower bed, with a wooden box on it, painted green.

"Tools and things in there," Johnnie said. "Here's my garden."

Sarah looked. Johnnie's garden was like all the others, just earth, nothing growing in it. Of course. It must have been quite different in the summer, with bright petunias blooming all over.

"They put some good earth in here for us," Johnnie was saying. "Feel it."

He reached over and dug his fingers into the earth. Sarah thought he would put some of the earth in her hand, the way his Aunt Ruth had, but instead he said, "Go on, Sarah, get close to the wall and dig in."

She moved closer, carefully, and dug the fingers of her left hand into the earth.

This earth had been warmed by the sun; it was loose and damp against her hand. Ruth would have said it was fertile soil. Sarah smiled at Johnnie.

"I've been putting in daffodil bulbs," he said. "How about planting one yourself? Or maybe two? They'd be just yours, and you could see them come up in the spring."

He was talking about spring as if she would be coming to Plainview again and again, and she was not sure she would be coming again at all.

But planting daffodil bulbs—she'd like that. Johnnie opened his tool box and took out a sharply pointed trowel and one brownish bulb.

"I only have one trowel," he said. "We can take turns."

He showed Sarah where to dig and started her hole for her. Then he handed her the trowel. Digging was harder than she expected. Her arm got tired, and then Johnnie took the trowel and dug a little. Whenever she said, *"All right?"* he said no, a daffodil hole had to be deeper.

At last he said the hole was deep enough, and she dropped the bulging bulb into it, with the growing end up, the way Johnnie showed her. He threw in a white powder he said was bone meal. Together they pushed earth back into the hole and pressed it down. Then Johnnie put a plastic marker next to where they had dug. "So we'll know that's *your* daffodil," he said.

Her daffodil. Maybe people with good arms and legs wouldn't think this was anything much, but it was one of the best things that had ever happened to her; she had dug a hole with her own hand and planted a bulb that would push leaves out of the earth in the springtime and make flowers.

She wondered if Johnnie understood that. He had said he meant to plant daffodils all around the edge of his garden.

As if in answer, he took her hand and brushed some earth off it. "I guess that's enough excitement for one day," he said. And it was. She turned to him with a smile.

On the way back, they paused at the bed of button chrysanthemums.

"Here, I'll get you a flower," Johnnie said. He leaned over, picked one stem full of blossoms, and handed it to Sarah. She took it in her hand and looked. Dozens of tiny, folded petals were gathered tight into each button blossom. Lovely.

"Thanks," she said, *"thanks, boy-J!"* And they laughed together.

The flowers fell onto her symbol board. "I'll put them in your buttonhole," Johnnie said. He reached over and carefully pulled the stem through the top buttonhole of her jacket. His eyes seemed to be smiling into hers. Sarah felt her face getting hot; she looked away.

"How did you like my garden?" Johnnie asked as they continued along the path, pausing when Sarah had something to say.

"Beautiful," Sarah said in symbols. *"I want a garden like that."*

"Come and live here, then," Johnnie said.

She shook her head. That was not at all what she had meant.

"Well, anyway," Johnnie said, "you can come to visit."

Sarah suddenly felt tears in her eyes. A thought had come to her—they had brought her here so she could see what an institution was like and so she would want to live here. Never, never!

All the way home that afternoon, she wondered.

"Did you have fun with Johnnie?" Ruth asked.

Yes. She nodded her head, *Oh, yes.*

"It's a beautiful place for those children," her mother said.

But not for me, Sarah was thinking. *Never.*

At supper, she was even more quiet than usual.

"What's the matter, Squib?" Amy wanted to know.

That was her sister, always knowing when something was wrong. Sarah wanted to tell her; Amy would understand. But not the others, not now.

"Nothing," she said.

Amy gave her a long look, not believing. But there was no chance to be alone with her sister that evening. A new friend of Amy's came over, and she and Amy watched television together. Sarah went into her room and practiced pointing at symbols, even the ones she knew and used every day.

Her mother came to put her to bed.

"We thought we gave you such a nice day," she said, "but you don't seem happy about it."

Sarah burst into tears. Her mother sat on the bed next to the wheelchair and put her arms around her. With her head nestled against her mother's shoulder, Sarah felt almost safe. Still, she cried.

"Tell me, Kitten," her mother said, and she helped

her sit up straight so she could point at symbols.

"*You want me to live in that house,*" Sarah said.

"What house?"

"*There. Today.*"

"Plainview? Oh Sarah, please, get that silly idea out of your head. We're not sending you away. Why would we, when you're doing so well here?"

Again Sarah felt herself in her mother's arms, comforted.

Her mother cried a little. "How wonderful," she said, "that you could tell me."

10

Edgar Meets His Match

I'm Arthur Gibson," the boy said. "We just moved in next door."

Amy had answered the bell, swinging the door wide. Now she just stood there. *Why doesn't she say something?* Sarah wondered as she steered her wheelchair towards the door. *Amy always knows what to say.* But maybe not to boys like Arthur. Sarah had never seen a boy like that. His hair was as blond as Ruth Burroughs', but his eyes were dark like Johnnie's and wide open. He waited, his big friendly smile slowly fading.

Sarah's mother appeared. "Come in, Arthur!" she exclaimed. "We're so glad to have someone next door."

It was easy after that. Sarah's mother introduced her daughters to Arthur and brought cranberry juice and cookies. It turned out that Arthur was just Amy's age, and she told him all about school. Sarah listened; now and then she made noises, not wanting to be left out.

Then Arthur turned to her and asked, "Have you been in a wheelchair very long?"

"She can't walk or talk," Amy said. "She has cerebral palsy."

Sarah banged on her symbol board, hard. There was Amy speaking *for* her, the way she did sometimes.

Arthur did not seem to care, though. He came right over and looked at Sarah's board. She pointed at the top of the board. "I communicate with Blissymbols," he read. "Show me, Sarah."

Sarah smiled at him, and he looked right into her eyes and smiled back. She felt warm all over, and she drew in her breath, fast.

She pointed again, and Arthur read the printed words out loud: "I am happy you are here."

Then Arthur tried pointing, slowly because he had to look for the words. "I want to be your friend."

"Terrific!" Amy exclaimed.

"What a neat way of saying things," Arthur said.

Then he wanted to know about her wheelchair. Could she go by herself?

Yes.

Even down the street?

Sarah shook her head. *No.*

Amy explained about Edgar. Sarah still didn't dare go down the street alone. No one knew what to do about Edgar.

When Amy had finished, Arthur turned to Sarah.

"Don't you worry," he said. "I'll take care of that Edgar, and then you can go down the street by yourself all you want."

Sarah gaped at him and blinked. "Agghh!" she said. She was astonished at this boy who seemed to think he could do anything.

Then he was leaving. "See you at the school bus in the morning," he said to Amy.

Toby appeared from somewhere and jumped onto Sarah's shoulder.

Something new is happening around here, Toby, she wanted to say.

Arthur really *was* different. It seemed to Sarah that he belonged to the world outside more than anyone else she knew, even Aunt Laura. Aunt Laura's world was somehow unreal. Of course there was Amy's world, and her father's, and in a way her mother's, but all that didn't count. They were family, and what she was thinking about was the world beyond her family, the world she was going to explore someday. In a wheelchair? People would surely ask her that. And she would tell them yes, in her own wheelchair. Just how she would do this she was not sure; she would see about that when the time came.

Meanwhile, she waited impatiently for Arthur to "take care of that Edgar." A week passed, and another. Sarah began to wonder if he was going to do anything at all. Then, just when she'd decided he'd forgotten, he turned up at the Bennetts' after school.

"You can go down the street, Sarah," he said. "I'll be watching."

Sarah looked up at him. He was so straight and strong. But she shook her head. *No.*

Arthur frowned. "Why not, Sarah? Don't you trust me?"

Actually, Sarah was not sure she *did* trust Arthur. How could she explain this in symbols? And where was he going to *be?*

Amy came to the rescue. "She has to know exactly where you'll be when she goes down the street," she told Arthur.

That's my sister, Sarah was thinking. *She knows just what's going on in my head and when to say it.*

"Okay," Arthur said. "I'll be right behind that big

lilac bush on the corner of our front yard nearest the Hoffmans' yard. How's that?"

Sarah nodded and pointed to her board. *"When?"*

"How about right now?"

"Is that boy (meaning Edgar) *home?"*

"I think so."

Arthur went out to hide behind the lilac bush. Amy said she would sit on the ramp in front and watch.

At last, Sarah started down the ramp and onto the sidewalk. She could hear her heart beating loudly inside her. She was scared.

Slowly, she made her way past the Gibsons' house. Sure enough, there was Arthur standing by the big lilac bush behind the hedge.

The bushes that used to lean across the walk in front of the Hoffman house were being trimmed. Edgar was there, clipping away at the bushes, lazily, as if he had all the time in the world. His back was towards her. He didn't look so terrible; anyway, not like someone who would knock over girls in wheelchairs. Sarah remembered how she had once admired that shaggy head of brown hair.

As he moved to the next bush, Edgar turned and saw her. Sarah tried to smile.

"I told you!" Edgar yelled at her. "I said not to come

here." He dropped his clippers and started towards her.

Keep going, Arthur had told her, keep going no matter what happens.

"Agghh," Sarah said in spite of herself.

Edgar ran up to the wheelchair and grabbed the handles at the back of it. At the same moment, Arthur bolted from behind the lilac bush and grabbed him around the waist. The next moment, Edgar was flat on the sidewalk.

Sarah turned her wheelchair around so she could watch. She had never seen such a ferocious fight. Edgar kicked and screamed. He got to his feet and tried punching. Arthur was lighter than Edgar; he could punch faster. Pretty soon, Edgar was down again, with blood pouring out of his nose. Arthur sat on his stomach and held his arms down.

"Mama!" Edgar screamed.

"You're going to let Sarah alone," Arthur said. "Promise?"

"Let me go!" Edgar squirmed and kicked some more.

"Promise?" Arthur repeated.

"Mama!"

"Promise?"

"I promise. Lemme go!"

Arthur stood up and wiped blood from his hands. "I guess he won't bother you anymore, Sarah," he said, and he turned and disappeared into his house. Amy, who had been watching close by, hesitated, then followed him.

Sarah felt sick to her stomach. All that blood. She had never seen so much blood.

Edgar just lay there, sniffling a little. His mother came calmly down the front walk, handed him a handkerchief for his bloody nose, and helped him get up. He limped a little. Slowly, with his mother's arm around his waist, he walked towards the house.

"Well, Edgar," his mother said, "this had to happen sometime."

Sarah's mother, on her way to see if Sarah needed help, said to no one in particular, "There go two wounded people."

11

More like
a Regular Girl

All right, now she could go down the street by herself. But the first time Sarah started off for school alone, she missed her mother. This surprised her. She had always tried to pretend her mother wasn't there, but now she knew that she had been aware of her mother's presence all the time, helping her to feel loved and secure. She wouldn't tell her mother, though. This was her chance to be on her own, and she didn't want anything to spoil it. Soon the trip became routine; she would leave for school early, looking back to make sure her mother wasn't following too closely. As for Edgar, she seldom saw him, except the few times when the high school bus was late and he would be waiting on the corner.

Sarah's mother had said she could go to the store by

herself, too. Since her wheelchair couldn't get through the door, she would wait outside until someone came by. The neighbors all knew her; someone would stop and ask what she wanted inside. Usually she would say, *"Ice cream."*

"A pop?"

"Yes, please," Sarah would reply, and she would reach into her pocket for her money.

Once she had an ice cream pop in her hand, she had to eat it sitting in front of the store because she couldn't hold a pop and work the wheelchair switch at the same time. That was all right. Sarah liked to watch people coming and going. Almost everyone would stop to exchange a few words with her.

At home Sarah said to her mother, *"I can go anywhere now. That boy-E. won't hurt me."*

"I'm glad," her mother said. "But I don't think being beat up helped Edgar to understand how he ought to treat people like you."

Sarah nodded. *"I don't like fights,"* she said.

"There should be a better way," her mother agreed. "But I don't know what anyone could have done about Edgar. His mother couldn't do anything. Or wouldn't; it's all the same."

Edgar's mother was so different from her own. Sarah

felt sorry for her. Mrs. Hoffman could walk and talk. She could do lots of other things. But she couldn't manage Edgar. It seemed she couldn't even manage herself very well.

Time passed. Colder days meant winter was coming. Sarah wore a sweater under her jacket when she went outside. School took up most of her time; it seemed better and better. She helped the other children with symbols, especially Joe, and before long she could listen to him read while Mrs. Stevens helped someone else. If he had trouble with a word she did not have on her symbol board, she would ask someone else to help—Jennifer, or sometimes her own mother; she didn't mind asking her for help now. Soon Joe would be reading as well as she did. And she herself was learning so much. She read more books than she ever had before, and she was pretty good at math and science. Now, too, she could write almost anything she wanted, slowly, carefully, with her good left hand. Even stories, and she liked that. She wrote stories at home, too.

Music class was a special time. The music teacher, Miss Carlson, came twice a week, bringing tambourines, triangles, bells that made all kinds of sounds, and a sort of wooden flute she said was a recorder.

Everyone sang, loud or soft, on pitch or not—except Sarah. But she could shake a tambourine or chime in with the bells when the teacher said, "Now, Sarah!" Between songs, Joe would sometimes play the recorder, blowing into one end and using his fingers on the holes. He said that he and his sister played duets with recorders at home.

All the songs were new to Sarah. They learned the tunes by singing them along with Miss Carlson, and sometimes she would play her guitar, too.

And now, Sarah even had a best friend—Maggie. They kept on doing tic-tac-toe on the playground, and Maggie invented a special handshake that they did when no one was looking, her right hand in Sarah's left one—two shakes down, then three more with their forefingers pointing up, in a special rhythm. This was magic, Maggie said; it meant they would be friends forever.

"*Always*," Sarah said, pointing to the symbol that came nearest to saying "forever." And she believed it.

Most of the children had lunch in the school cafeteria. Sarah asked Maggie about it. "I eat with a couple of girls in my class," Maggie said. "It's noisy. You're lucky you can go home."

Sarah wanted Maggie to come to her house after

school. And sure enough, one blowy November day Maggie appeared at the door of Sarah's classroom just as school was ending.

"I can walk home with you if you want," she said. "Then I can take the bus on the corner to my house."

Wonderful, Sarah thought. Having a friend come home with her from school made her even more like a regular girl.

"Can't stay long, have to get home before dark," Maggie went on.

Oh yes, days were shorter now. Sarah pointed at "Okay," and then she and Maggie did their special handshake together.

Sarah usually did not start for home until most of the children were on their way and the sidewalks were fairly clear. This time, she and Maggie set out right away, with Maggie going first, calling out now and then, "Hey, look out, kids!"

It was so different from other times. Little groups of girls walked by, chatting. Sarah loved to see the various styles of their jeans, so tight in the rear she didn't see how they could sit. Hers were not tight; sitting all day in a wheelchair made that uncomfortable. But it didn't matter; no one ever got to see her behind.

Children kept rushing past, the boys almost always

in more of a hurry than the girls. A boy called out, "Hi, Sarah!" as she went by. And another, "Hi, Maggie!"

Sarah's mother always left school a little early; she wanted to be home for Sarah. This time she welcomed Maggie, too. But once they were settled in the big living room, Sarah was not sure what they were going to do.

Maggie decided that. "Look!" she said. "Let's make up a story with symbols. First you make a sentence, then I make one. I'll pretend I can't talk, and I'll point at symbols just the way you do. Any symbols I don't know yet, I can read the words to myself."

Sarah banged her wheelchair tray with approval. Maggie moved a chair up close to Sarah so she could reach the symbols. Soon they were making up a sort of story, taking turns and laughing hilariously. Neither Sarah nor Maggie could remember enough of it afterwards to write it down.

Amy came bouncing in, rosy-cheeked from the cold. "You've got a new friend, Squib!" she exclaimed.

They all had a snack with Sarah's mother—hot chocolate and cinnamon doughnuts.

After that, Maggie came at least once a week. She and Sarah found plenty to do. Sometimes they played rock music on Sarah's tape player. Amy would stop by to listen, too.

"Maggie's a nice girl," Sarah's mother said. "I'm glad she comes home with you."

"*Yes*," Sarah said. "*I have a friend*." And she meant a friend who walks on two legs and talks, like most of the people in the world.

❉ ❉ ❉

When the days started to get even colder, Ruth Burroughs said to Sarah, "You won't be out in the garden so often now. I'll miss you."

Sarah pointed. "*Come to my house*."

Ruth nodded. "Okay, sometimes. But I want you to come to *my* house. Maybe Harry can make a ramp for the back steps."

Sarah let out a joyful squeal. At last, she might be seeing Ruth at home, in her own kitchen.

Harry Burroughs did make a ramp, sawing and hammering with Sarah's father, just as they had when they made ramps for the van and for the Bennetts' back steps. This one could be put in the Burroughs' basement when it was not in use.

Then, one afternoon when Sarah was sitting in the garden, Ruth leaned over the fence and said, "I'm going to be working at the library, Sarah. Only home alone Mondays. That's when I would have plenty of time for you."

Only Mondays? Sarah was thinking. *Well, all right, Mondays.*

"Please," Ruth said to Sarah's mother, "let me have Sarah Monday afternoons. My house is so empty without children."

Sarah's mother agreed gratefully, and after that Sarah would head straight for Ruth's house after school on Mondays, up the ramp at the back, and through the door Ruth held open for her with a welcoming smile.

Sarah could not remember being in any kitchen except her own. She had no idea that kitchens could be so different. Stoves and refrigerators surely had to be white, but—imagine!—these were green. Cabinets, instead of being all brown, were painted in pale colors—yellow, blue, green, and a lovely lavender. Curtains at the windows were covered all over with yellow flowers and green leaves. Sarah thought she had never seen anything so beautiful.

One Monday they made cupcakes. Sarah stirred the batter, her good hand grasping the handle of a big wooden spoon. Another Monday they just talked, and both of them made funny drawings with symbols in them.

Sarah wanted Toby with her on these Monday afternoons. She did not have a picture of him on her board, but she had made sure there was a symbol for "cat." She pointed to it.

Ruth laughed. "Do you want Toby? I'll go get him."

Some Monday afternoons Ruth would borrow the Bennetts' van, and they would go to visit Johnnie at Plainview. Sarah had not been sure she wanted to go again, but anything Ruth planned for Monday afternoons was all right with her.

Johnnie always seemed glad to see her. Ruth would leave them alone for part of the time, and they would go out to the gardens because there was hardly anybody else there this time of year.

One time, she met Johnnie's mother there, a little woman with dark hair wound around her head in a braid. She gave Sarah a picture of Johnnie, just the right size for her symbol board. Sarah's mother pasted it on the board, in the row with the other pictures. *My family and Ruth Burroughs, and now Johnnie,* Sarah thought. *Like having a brother.*

"Remember," Johnnie would say, "anytime you come, I can talk for you. I can be your voice."

Another time Johnnie said there was going to be a concert on Saturday. A man was going to sing in the gym. Could she come? Ruth could not go; she worked on Saturdays. But Sarah's mother said she'd take her; she'd like to see Johnnie again.

Sarah asked Amy if she'd go, too, but Amy said, "Sorry, Squib, I'd like to meet your Johnnie but I'm going roller skating with Arthur."

"And you?" Sarah tried to say to her father, who had been reading the paper while he waited for supper. She rang her bell so he would look. *"And you? Will you come with us on Saturday?"*

"It's time you did, Tom," her mother said. "You haven't been on a trip with us for months."

"I'll think about it," he said, and Sarah guessed that was all the answer she would get.

Later, when Sarah was alone with her mother, she said, *"Why doesn't Father want to go with us?"*

"Maybe he will go this time," her mother answered, and she sighed. "Try to understand, Kitten. It *is* hard for him. He wanted so much for you to be an active healthy daughter."

"Like Amy?"

"Not like Amy, just yourself."

They were both quiet for a while.

Then, "Sometimes," Sarah's mother said, "your father wonders why this had to happen to *his* daughter.

146

IIe feels like running away."

"Do you *feel like that?"* Sarah wanted to know.

"Never, Kitten. You're special to me."

Sarah remembered when Amy had said that.

"Your father *does* love you," her mother went on. "It's just a bit different for him, that's all."

She put her arms around her daughter and they held each other tight.

There were three days before the trip. Nobody talked about it. Sarah wanted to ask her father again if he'd go, but she was afraid she would cry if he said no. She did not want him to know she cared that much.

Then came the big surprise. They had just started lunch on the day of the trip when Sarah's father said to her, "Do you still want me to go to Plainview with you?"

Sarah's soup spoon clattered to the floor. She nodded her head hard. *Yes!*

"What about your ball game?" her mother asked. "The Hawks and the Hares?"

"Well. . ." her father began. There was a long pause. "It was cancelled."

"Oh."

"But I really do want to go. I've been hearing about Johnnie, and I want to do more things with Sarah." He stood there, just looking down at the floor.

Sarah did not know what to make of all this. "Agghh!" she said.

"You'll see," her father said quietly. "Things will be different."

✳ ✳ ✳

All the way to Plainview, Sarah kept saying to herself, *This is special, special. My father is coming to Plainview!*

Johnnie was waiting for them at the big front door.

"Happy day!" he said to Sarah's father when her mother had introduced them. "I've been hoping you'd come. Sarah has told me so much about you."

Sarah's father cleared his throat and looked away, without saying anything. *He wonders what I said to Johnnie,* Sarah was thinking, and she tried to remember when she had ever talked to Johnnie about her father at all.

The concert was about to begin. Johnnie led them into a huge room where children of many sizes and ages had gathered, most of them in wheelchairs, some able to propel themselves by hand or with a motor, others being pushed.

A man with a bushy brown beard, holding a guitar, stood at one end of the room. He said his name was Joe.

148

Then he talked to them, played the guitar with quick fingers, and sang some songs Sarah had never heard before.

"Kum ba ya, my Lord, kum ba ya...

Someone's crying, Lord, kum ba ya!"

What did the strange words mean? Answering her unspoken question, Joe said, "Those words come from Africa. They mean 'Come by here.' "

Someone's crying, Lord, Sarah repeated to herself. *These children must cry sometimes, just as I do. They need someone to sing to them. They need God to come by here.*

More songs, finally the one Ruth Burroughs sang to her, about an answer blowing in the wind. Everyone listened, no one said a word.

Then, songs for everyone to join in, if they could. And something called a round. Joe told children in various parts of the room to start singing when he waved his hand at them. And they did, singing "Row, row, row your boat, Gently down the stream. . . ," each group starting at a different time but somehow all together.

No one here could ever row a boat, Sarah was thinking. It didn't matter; it was just a song.

Sarah's mother and father both joined in when their turn came.

Sarah, too: "Agghh! Agghh!"

"Not you, Sarah," Johnnie whispered to her, and she was not sure she liked him after all.

Sarah's father had heard. He moved close, put an arm around her shoulder, and said, "You sing all you want, Sarah. *I* like to hear you."

Sarah shook her head in amazement and looked up into her father's eyes. The wonder of it; her own father had said that, her own father liked to hear her sing.

All the way home she was singing inside herself.

12

Sing for Me, Johnnie

Winter came early that year, and hard. Snow blocked the streets and drifted deep against the house. Some days the schools were closed. When they were open, Sarah's mother would push the wheelchair down the snowy street, bumping along, stopping to rest now and then. Sarah herself could not make the wheelchair go in the snow; pushing the switch just made the wheels spin.

No one even talked about going to Plainview until January, when an unexpected thaw melted some of the snow, and the streets were clear.

"I wondered when you could get here," Johnnie said as he greeted Sarah and Ruth. "It's a long winter."

They could not go out to the gardens, so Johnnie took Sarah to the room he shared with another boy,

Kevin, on the third floor. Johnnie could work the elevator himself; its door opened when he pushed a switch on his wheelchair. This seemed like magic to Sarah.

The room was bright and neat, with shelves for Johnnie's special possessions. But it was small; their two wheelchairs took up most of Johnnie's part of the room. Sarah wondered how Johnnie managed when Kevin was there. Kevin was away now, Johnnie had said, visiting his uncle.

"In a wheelchair?" Sarah had asked in symbols.

"In a wheelchair," Johnnie said, "like me."

The walls of the room were decorated with big colorful posters of athletes—football, baseball, tennis, hockey players. Sarah was not sure which were Johnnie's and which Kevin's. She looked and looked. All those sports that Johnnie could only watch, never take part in himself.

Sarah turned to see what Johnnie kept on the shelves in his corner of the room. A whole row of books; he must like to read as much as she did. A collection of little model cars on another shelf. Cars were for going places. Kevin had gone to visit his uncle. What about Johnnie?

Johnnie was watching her symbol board, as if he wanted her to say something. *"Johnnie, do you go home sometimes?"* Sarah asked him.

"Now and then," Johnnie said, "when my mother's not too busy. But this is really home."

This is really home, Sarah repeated to herself. She wanted so much to know more about Johnnie.

About his father—*"Does your father come to see you, Johnnie?"*

"Not anymore."

Sarah put her hand on his. *"I'm sorry."*

"So am I. But I don't think he ever liked me much."

Johnnie's father—he wasn't even there. Not like her father, who came home to his family every night, and loved them all.

Sarah glanced at Johnnie again and then looked away because there were tears in his eyes. On the wall above his bed she saw a big framed symbol, one she did not remember:

What was he doing with Blissymbols? She pointed to that symbol and made questioning sounds.

"The speech teacher gave me that," Johnnie said. "It means 'peace,' the kind you feel inside yourself. We need that."

Sarah nodded.

"She showed me how this symbol was made," Johnnie went on. "Heart for feeling—you know that.

And of course the line below is for the earth and the one above for the sky. So it means a feeling of belonging to the whole world, earth and sky together."

That was peace. That was what she felt sometimes as she lay in bed in the early morning, waiting for her mother. *Peace to you, Johnnie. Peace to all of us.*

"Remember when we went to sing in the gym?" Johnnie was saying. And he sang that song for her: "Kum ba ya!" In spite of herself Sarah joined in: "Agghh!" But this time he did not tell her to stop.

"It's all right, Sarah," he said when they were finished. "I know that's all the voice you have."

Sarah pointed at the symbols on her board. *Sing for me, Johnnie,* she wanted to say to him. *Be my voice.*

But he was not looking.

* * *

No winter lasts forever, and this time spring was especially welcome. The snow in the streets melted and sent little rivulets running down the gutters and gurgling into the sewers. Days were longer; there was more than an hour of daylight after Sarah got home from school. On Mondays she and Ruth Burroughs would look for the purple and white crocuses Ruth had planted in the fall. When the right day came, the flowers would burst open in the sunlight. Green shoots of daffodil leaves were pushing out of the wet soil. Toby joyfully scratched in the earth and squatted, free of his litter box at last. He was a big cat now, no longer a kitten.

As she always had, Sarah would lie in bed in the early morning and listen, until her mother came. Outdoor sounds were very different in different seasons. Winter was mostly silent, with windows kept shut against the cold. But now she could hear those lazy bird-peeps in the tree outside her window. The robins had come back; she had seen one in the garden the day before.

Indoor sounds did not change so much. There was a clatter of dishes in the kitchen, then the sound of water pouring into the teakettle, followed by a slight clang as it was put on the stove. That was her mother getting breakfast.

Curled against her legs on the blanket, Toby stirred, stretched his whole body, and yawned. Then he pulled himself up and walked daintily up the bed while Sarah kept saying "Agghh, agghh!" He knew these were welcoming sounds. Purring, he made kneading motions against her chest with his paws. Toby could not talk any more than she could. But she knew what he meant when he purred. This was the kind of love that asked no questions and needed no words.

There was a tapping now at her window, as if some-one wanted to get in. That was a long branch of the maple tree, pushed by the wind. Often she would wake in the night to the sound of that tapping. In the dark-ness this seemed to her like a message from another world.

Sometimes as she lay awake, she felt more and more certain that there was a world out there she could never quite explore or understand. Not the everyday world of family and friends and school—that she would keep on exploring. But another world, often scary, that spoke to her in the tapping of the branch and showed itself in her dreams. Perhaps, after all, this was a world inside herself, and in other people, too. Perhaps that was where God was.

She could not tell her mother how she felt about this other world. It would be hard to explain, even if she could talk. Even harder in symbols, though someday she would try. She was learning, all the time, how to say more in symbols. To her they were a real language. Someday, too, she might write in words about this world inside herself.

In her daydreams she imagined a person who would be so close to her that thoughts like these would be understood without words. Maybe, when she was older, a young man.

She had had daydreams about this young man ever since Arthur had taken Amy to a school dance in the fall. Amy had looked lovely, in a long, pale blue dress with ruffles around her shoulders.

"You're growing up," her mother had said.

"Of course," Amy said, and she went to answer the doorbell.

Sarah had always thought Arthur was handsome, but that night he seemed to her so beautiful that she drew in her breath quickly and blinked. He had let his blond hair grow almost to his shoulders, and his eyes seemed darker than ever.

"For the prettiest girl in town," he said as he handed Amy a single red rose.

Then he turned to Sarah. "You're a pretty girl, too," he told her. "I should have brought you a flower."

Sarah smiled and smiled, wanting at least to say thank you, but there was no time; Arthur and Amy hurried off to the dance.

He had said she was pretty; she treasured those words. Maybe someday another boy, walking tall and straight as Arthur, would tell her she was pretty and even take her to a school dance. Maybe. She wouldn't mind just watching the others dance.

She wanted to be as pretty as she could be, every day. Amy gave her a lipstick, and Sarah practiced making her lips rosy-red. It was hard, with her wobbly hand, not to make it smeary.

"Am I pretty?" she asked Amy.

"Of course," Amy said. That was her answer to nearly everything these days.

"Amy has Arthur for a friend, and you have Johnnie," her mother commented.

Yes, there was Johnnie. She could visit him more often, now that it was spring. Sometimes her mother took her to Plainview on a Saturday. Sarah wondered at Johnnie's wanting her to come. He was nearly fifteen years old—Amy's age—and in his first year at a regular high school. He went to school in a van with other children, the way she had gone to Ingleside.

There was a Saturday when Sarah's mother left her at Plainview while she went to visit a friend who lived nearby. Sarah found Johnnie alone in his wheelchair in a corner of the big lounge at Plainview. *He's too quiet,* she thought. But when he saw Sarah he smiled and moved his wheelchair close to hers so he could see her symbol board.

"Garden today?" Sarah asked.

Johnnie shook his head, "No, not today. Let's stay inside."

Here it was, a warm spring day, breezes blowing, bright flowers under the sun, and Johnnie wanted to stay inside. What could be the matter?

"Don't you feel well?"

"It's not that," Johnnie said. "Sometimes I just get to thinking about things."

What things? Sarah wondered to herself.

"Is high school hard?" she asked.

"Lots of things are hard. Growing up is hard. Being a teenager is hard."

Johnnie banged on the arm of his wheelchair. "It's these terrible legs, this wanting to walk around like anyone else!"

He was shouting. Someone turned up the rock music on a nearby radio.

Sarah knew about growing up. It *was* hard. Being a teenager must be even harder. She wanted to give Johnnie a hug but she didn't dare, he was shaking so. Finally she touched his arm so he would look at her symbol board.

"Johnnie," she said. *"I want to help."*

Johnnie grinned sheepishly. He had never before complained to Sarah like this.

"Just come as often as you can," he said. "We can help each other."

"*I'll come,*" she assured him. "*But don't you have friends here, too?*"

"I have friends here. But you're special, Sarah. I knew that the very first time you came."

It wasn't easy to respond to that the way she wanted. She paused, and then said quickly with symbols, "*I am happy with you, Johnnie.*"

And Johnnie: "I am happy with you, too."

13

Thirteen Candles

Sarah was to have a real party for her birthday in April. It was the first time. Before that, the only people at Sarah's birthday were her family and Ruth Burroughs. That didn't make a real party.

Sarah's mother had said she could invite some friends. Wonderful, Sarah thought; she'd have her whole class from school—and Maggie, and Johnnie.

"Not your whole class!" her mother exclaimed.

"*Oh.*" Sarah had been so sure they would come. After all, there were only seven children in her class, besides herself. Of course, Maggie and Johnnie would make nine.

Sarah looked up at her mother's face. She was tired, and no wonder. She didn't need seven more "special" children in her house—besides Maggie and Johnnie.

"All right." Sarah said this by raising her arm, and then her mother looked at her board. *"Mama, I want Johnnie. And Maggie."*

So Johnnie would be guest of honor at the party for Sarah's thirteenth birthday. He would come to her house for the first time, in the Plainview van.

Maggie would come, too, though she had said she "wasn't much good at parties."

Sarah woke up early that morning. Her mother came almost as early.

"Happy birthday, Kitten!" She kissed Sarah, then combed her hair and tied a bright red ribbon in it.

Amy appeared, giggling. "Poppa says there's a big surprise for you, Squib!"

"Don't talk about it," her mother said. "She has to wait until the party."

Sarah wondered how she could possibly wait that long.

"Anyway, you can have my present now," Amy said, and she put a flat, square box wrapped in flowery paper on Sarah's bed.

Sarah did her own giggle for Amy: "G-g-g-g."

Amy unwrapped the box and opened it. There was a square metal board with a bright-colored pattern printed on it that looked like a path wandering around, and some round pieces with numbers on them that stuck to it.

"It's a game," Amy said. "We can play it together. Maggie, too. The board can go on your wheelchair tray. The counters stick to it with magnets."

Sarah loved Amy for thinking of a game like that. She put her good arm on Amy's shoulder and patted her gently.

There was another package at Sarah's place at breakfast, from her mother. It was tied with a wide blue ribbon and wrapped loosely so Sarah could undo it herself. A book: *The Hobbit*.

"Make believe," her mother said. "The kind you like."

Sarah made grateful noises and blew a kiss to her mother, who was making pancakes at the stove.

"Just wait until you see my surprise," Sarah's father said.

"Can't wait."

"You'll have to; I want everyone to be here. It's something really special."

The pancakes were heaped on plates now. Sarah's father poured maple syrup on hers until the pancakes swam in it.

"Any ball game today?" Amy asked her father, and

Sarah wondered why she brought *that* up.

"Not today. How could I miss Sarah's party?"

The rest of the morning was uneventful. Soon after lunch Aunt Laura arrived, bearing a big, square bakery box.

"Is that the surprise?" Sarah wanted to know.

"It's a surprise, all right," Aunt Laura said.

"But not *the* surprise," Amy said. "Anyone can see that's a cake."

"You *are* a killjoy," Aunt Laura complained.

Then the doorbell rang; Amy opened the door, and Johnnie came right into the house as if he had done it a dozen times before. Sarah caught a glimpse of the van that had brought him, just starting back down the street.

Amy was standing in the doorway.

"You must be Sarah's sister!" Johnnie said.

"Johnnie!" Amy exclaimed. "I've wanted to meet you for the longest time."

Then why didn't you go to Plainview with us? Sarah was thinking.

Never mind. Johnnie smiled at Sarah and handed her a bunch of daffodils so big that it took most of her arm to hold them.

"You should come to see *your* daffodils; they're

blooming in my garden," he said.

Sarah made welcoming sounds and pointed to *"Thank you, thank you, friend Johnnie."*

Then Johnnie was welcomed by Sarah's father and mother, and introduced to Aunt Laura. Sarah's mother put the daffodils in water in the biggest vase she had.

Maggie arrived a little late, breathless. In spite of what Maggie had said, Sarah thought that she *would* be "good at parties," though perhaps she felt uneasy with people she didn't know. There were three here— Sarah's father, Aunt Laura, and Johnnie. When she was introduced to each of them, Maggie shook hands rather stiffly and repeated, "How do you do?"

All this time Maggie had been holding her present for Sarah, cradling it against herself with her left arm. Now she put it down carefully on Sarah's wheelchair tray.

"You can undo the ribbon yourself, Sarah," she said. "I tied it that way. Just pull one end."

Sarah pulled. The yellow ribbon came off, and Maggie helped her remove the tissue paper. A square box, not too big for Sarah's hand. She grasped the cover and pulled it off.

There inside was a round, gold-colored metal box with a handle on top. Sarah lifted it out by the handle and set it carefully on her tray.

"Now I'll have to show you," Maggie said. "This is a music box. You can hold it in place and push the switch all with one hand. I tried it, so I know it works."

Sarah watched. Everyone else watched, too. Maggie pushed a little switch on the top of the box, and the top started going around and a sweet, tinkly tune came out of the box.

What a wonderful present. Sarah made her giggling sounds, "G-g-g," and patted Maggie on the shoulder.

Maggie turned the switch off and let Sarah do it herself. Tinkly tune.

"When it winds all the way down someone will have to wind it up for you," Maggie said. "But you can do the rest."

Ruth Burroughs came, bringing pretty blue pants and a shirt she had made for Sarah. The shirt fastened down the front with velcro, like the blouse she had made before.

Sarah gave Ruth a hug with her good arm.

Amy had invited Arthur. He brought a big box of chocolates wrapped in silver paper.

"For a lovely birthday girl," he said, while Amy opened the box for Sarah. Sarah looked inside. Big, luscious, creamy-brown chocolates, row after row. Amy passed them around, to Sarah first, and everyone had one.

Then Amy and Arthur went downstairs to play Ping-Pong. They came back up just in time for cake and ice cream.

"Well," Aunt Laura commented, "it seems you are with us, after all."

Sarah's mother brought in the cake, with candle flames flickering, and set it on the table in front of Sarah while everyone sang Happy Birthday. Such a cake! It was big and round, with white lettering on chocolate frosting: Happy Birthday dear Sarah. Thirteen pink lighted candles surrounded this message. Then there were red roses all around the edge, with pink and green leaves in between.

They were all waiting for her to blow out the candles. You have to be a good blower to do that, with strong muscles around your mouth, and it takes a big push to get the air going. Sarah had practiced this for a long time, and most of that time she thought she could never do it. Her mother had helped. For several weeks before the party, she would light a single candle after supper, and Sarah would blow and blow. Whuff! At last the candle did go out; she could do it after all.

Now, thirteen candles. She drew in her breath and

pushed it out, fast. All the candles blew out except one. Everyone clapped.

"Bravo!" her father exclaimed.

"Marvelous, Squib!"

"I didn't know you could do that," Johnnie said. More than anyone else, he knew how much this meant to Sarah.

She had certainly changed. Blowing out candles was one small way of showing it. Sarah remembered how she had expected to be a baby forever, with her mother to take care of her. Now, the worst thing she could think of would be to just sit and let other people do things for her.

Time to cut the cake. Sarah cut one piece, slowly, her hand wobbling with anticipation. Aunt Laura cut the rest and gave some to everyone. It was as delicious as it was beautiful, Sarah thought—a yellow cake with all those trimmings, and raspberry jam in the middle. Sarah had a whole rose on her piece. And of course, there was ice cream.

Toby had hidden under the sofa in all the excitement, but now he came out and jumped onto Sarah's shoulder. She gave him part of her rose.

But where was that big surprise, she wondered? Just then, her father slipped quietly out of the room. Soon he came back carrying a heavy-looking grey plastic box with a pink ribbon tied to it.

"What's *that?*" Amy said.

Sarah gaped and blinked. What had her father thought up this time?

He put the box on the table, took off its cover, and set on Sarah's wheelchair tray a shining new typewriter.

"AGGHH!" she fairly screamed. She had tried a typewriter once at school, but this one looked much better.

"Marvelous, Squib!" Amy was saying again.

"Now you can write stories faster," Johnnie said.

"She can't type all that fast with only one hand," Aunt Laura commented.

It was like Aunt Laura to say something like that, Sarah thought. Never mind— she could type much faster with one hand than she could do handwriting.

"This is an electric typewriter," Sarah's father said to her. "The keys will be easy for you to push. Your mother can teach you how to use it."

"Me?" Sarah's mother exclaimed. "It's been years since I've used a typewriter, and I never was much good at it."

Aunt Laura had been looking the typewriter over curiously.

"Well," she said. "I guess this is where *I* come in. I used to work on a typewriter like this every day, before I got my computer. *I* can teach Sarah."

Sarah had been wondering how she could learn to use this beautiful machine. Aunt Laura to the rescue! She would be so patient if Aunt Laura would teach her. She wouldn't even care if Aunt Laura got mad.

Sarah's symbol board was completely covered by the typewriter, so she could not say any of this. She kept nodding her head, *yes, yes.* She wanted to hug her father for giving her such a wonderful present, but when she tried to steer her wheelchair close to him, he had somehow moved away.

Her father. He loved her, but when she needed him, she could not quite be sure he'd be there.

"Come on over by the wall, Sarah," he was saying. "I'll plug this in for you."

Of course, Sarah told herself. Her father hadn't meant to move away; he'd been getting ready to plug in her typewriter. She moved over near the wall. Her father unwound the cord and pushed the plug into an outlet. Then he put a piece of paper into the typewriter and showed Sarah the switch.

"This *is* too big for your wheelchair," he said. "We'll set it up for you on your desk. But you can try typing on it right now."

Sarah nodded again, moved closer, and poked away, spelling her name while everyone watched. Then, slowly, she typed out, "Thank you everyone for this lovely party."

Everyone gave a spontaneous cheer.

"This is the best party I've ever been to!" That was Maggie.

"You just wait, Sarah," Johnnie said. "Now you've got a typewriter. Someday you may get a word processor or a computer."

Sarah didn't know much about such things, but she nodded at Johnnie as if to say *Yes, yes, why not?*

"Happy day Squib," Amy said, and this seemed the last word on Sarah's party.

Later, after her mother had put her to bed, Sarah lay awake in the quiet darkness, thinking about the people at her party.

First of all, her father. He had given her important things over the years—a wheelchair she could work by herself, a van to go places in, an electric typewriter today. Giving was his way of showing love; she ought to remember that.

Then, the others. Those she could depend on the most—her mother and Amy, Ruth Burroughs, and

Maggie, who promised to be her friend as long as she lived. Nothing to worry about when she thought of them, just a good, warm feeling.

Aunt Laura, who brought the beautiful cake with roses all around. That was *her* way. And now, wonder of wonders, it was Aunt Laura who would teach her how to use the new typewriter.

Johnnie. He would never come to her walking on two legs, never take her to a dance. But she could never walk to him, either, and of course, she couldn't dance.

Johnnie was real. As he was leaving the party, he had moved his wheelchair close to hers, put his right hand over her left one, and held it tight.

"Come as soon as you can," he said. "Remember, I can be your voice."

Johnnie; he was just one of the great people in her world. As she drifted off to sleep, she loved them all.

Afterword

In 1967, when Elizabeth Helfman wrote a book called *Signs and Symbols Around the World*, she had no idea she would help change the way a lot of people communicate. In her book, she told about Charles Bliss, an Australian man whose new system of symbols was designed for international communication. At the Hugh Macmillan Rehabilitation Centre in Toronto, Canada, some teachers read Ms. Helfman's book and learned about that system. Surely this was just what children who could not speak needed. The children learned first a few symbols, then more and more, until they could truly say, "Symbols do what talking does."

Ms. Helfman and her book proved to be a vital link between Mr. Bliss and the many people who needed his symbols. Thanks in part to Elizabeth Helfman's work, people like Sarah Bennett now have a way to communicate—through Blissymbols. They can ask questions and can tell the world what is on their minds. This has meant for them a whole new way of thinking and feeling.

On Being Sarah is based on the life of a real girl. It is one of a number of Elizabeth Helfman's writings that deal with the choices and challenges of people who use alternatives to oral speech.